WAITING FOR ANYA

Other books by Michael Morpurgo

Friend or Foe
King of the Cloud Forests
Little Foxes
Long Way Home
Mr Nobody's Eyes
My Friend Walter
The Nine Lives of Montezuma
Twist of Gold
War Horse
The War of Jenkins' Ear
The White Horse of Zennor
Why the Whales Came
The Wreck of the Zanzibar

for younger readers

Conker
Colly's Barn
The Marble Crusher
The Sandman and the Turtles
Snakes and Ladders

Waiting for Anya

Michael Morpurgo

MAMMOTH

First published in Great Britain 1990
by William Heinemann Ltd
Published 1991 by Mammoth
an imprint of Reed Consumer Books Limited
Michelin House, 81 Fulham Road, London SW3 6RB
and Auckland, Melbourne, Singapore and Toronto

Reprinted 1991, 1992 (twice), 1993 (twice),
1994 (twice), 1995

Copyright © 1990 by Michael Morpurgo

ISBN 0 7497 0634 1

A CIP catalogue record for this title
is available from the British Library

Printed and bound in Great Britain
by Cox & Wyman Ltd, Reading, Berkshire

For Séverine
who helped so much with this book.

My thanks also to Jo Coustère, Jean Coustère, Gilberte Tintorère; to François Trésaricq former Mayor of Lescun and to Madame Trésaricq; to Dominique Cruhapecascade, shepherd, also of Lescun; and to Laurent Asserquet Lapassat.

Chapter One

Jo should have known better. After all Papa had told him often enough: 'Whittle a stick Jo, pick berries, eat, look for your eagle if you must,' he'd said, 'but do something. You sit doing nothing on a hillside in the morning sun with the tinkle of sheep bells all about you and you're bound to drop off. You've got to keep your eyes busy, Jo. If your eyes are busy then they won't let your brain go to sleep. And whatever you do, Jo, never lie down. Sit down but don't lie down.' Jo knew all that, but he'd been up since half past five that morning and milked a hundred sheep. He was tired, and anyway the sheep seemed settled enough grazing the pasture below him. Rouf lay beside him, his head on his paws, watching the sheep. Only his eyes moved.

Jo lay back on the rock and considered the lark rising above him and wondered why larks seem to perform when the sun shines. He could hear the church bells of Lescun in the distance but only faintly. Lescun, his village, his valley, where the people lived for their sheep and their cows. And they lived with them too. Half of each house was given over to the animals, a dairy on the ground floor, a hay loft above; and in front of every house was a walled yard that served as a permanent sheep fold.

For Jo the village was his whole world. He'd only been out of it a few times in all his twelve years, and one of those was to the railway station just two years before to see his father off to the war. They'd all gone, all the men who weren't too young and who weren't too old. It wouldn't take long to hammer the Boche and they'd be back home again. But when the news had come it had all been bad, so bad you couldn't believe it. There were rumours first of retreat and then of defeat, of French armies disintegrating, of English armies driven into the sea. Jo did not believe any of it at first, nor did anyone; but then one morning outside the Mairie he saw Grandpère crying openly in the street and he had to believe it. Then they heard that Jo's father was a prisoner-of-war in Germany and so were all the others who had gone from the village; except Jean Marty, cousin Jean, who would never be coming back. Jo lay there and tried to picture Jean's face; he could not. He could remember his dry cough though and the way he would spring down a mountain like a deer. Only Hubert could run faster than Jean. Hubert Sarthol was the giant of the village. He had the mind of a child and could only speak a few recognisable words. The rest of his talk was a miscellany of grunting and groaning and squeaking but somehow he managed to make himself more or less understood. Jo remembered how Hubert had cried when they told him he couldn't join the army like the others. The bells of Lescun and the bells of the sheep blended in soporific harmony to lull him away into his dreams.

Rouf was the kind of dog that didn't need to bark too often. He was a massive white mountain dog, old and stiff in his legs but still top dog in the village and he knew it. He was barking now though, a gruff roar of a bark that woke Jo instantly. He sat up. The sheep were gone. Rouf roared again from somewhere behind him, from in among the trees. The sheep bells were loud with alarm, their cries shrill and strident. Jo was on his feet and whistling for Rouf to bring them back. They scattered out of the wood and came running and leaping down towards him. Jo thought it was a lone sheep at first that had got itself caught up on the edge of the wood, but then it barked as it backed away and became Rouf – Rouf rampant, hackles up, snarling; and there was blood on his side. Jo ran towards him calling him back and it was then that he saw the bear and stopped dead. As the bear came out into the sunlight she stood up, her nose lifted in the air. Rouf stayed his ground, his body shaking with fury as he barked.

The nearest Jo had ever been to a bear before was

to the bearskin that hung on the wall in the café. Stood up as she was she was as tall as a full-grown man, her coat a creamy brown, her snout black. Jo could not find his voice to shout with, he could not find his legs to run with. He stood mesmerised, quite unable to take his eyes off the bear. A terrified ewe blundered into him and knocked him over. Then he was on his feet, and without even a look over his shoulder he was running down towards the village. He careered down the slopes, his arms flailing to keep his balance. Several times he tumbled and rolled and picked himself up again, but as he gathered speed his legs would run away with him once more. All it needed was a rock or a tussock of grass to send him sprawling once again. Bruised and bloodied he reached the track to the village and ran, legs pumping, head back, and shouting whenever he could find the breath to do it.

By the time he reached the village – and never had it taken so long – he hadn't the breath to say more than one word, but one word was all he needed. 'Bear!' he cried and pointed back to the mountains, but he had to repeat it several times before they seemed to understand or perhaps before they would believe him. Then his mother had him by the shoulders and was trying to make herself heard through the hubbub of the crowd about them.

'Are you all right, Jo? Are you hurt?' she said.

'Rouf, Maman,' he gasped. 'There's blood all over him.'

'The sheep,' Grandpère shouted. 'What about

10

the sheep?'

Jo shook his head. 'I don't know,' he said. 'I don't know.'

Monsieur Sarthol, Hubert's father and mayor of the village as long as Jo had been alive, was trying to organise loudly; but no-one was paying him much attention. They had gone for their guns and for their dogs. Within minutes they were all gathered in the Square, some on horseback but most on foot. Those children that could be caught were shut indoors in the safekeeping of grandmothers, mothers or aunts; but many escaped their clutches and dived unseen into the narrow streets to join up with the hunting party as it left the village. A bear hunt was once in a lifetime and not to be missed. This was the stuff of legends and here was one in the making. Jo pleaded with Grandpère to be allowed to go but Grandpère could do nothing for him, Maman would have none of it. He was bleeding profusely from his nose and his knee, so despite all his objections he was bustled away into the house to have his wounds cleaned and bandaged. Christine, his small sister, gazed up at him with big eyes as Maman wiped away the blood.

'Where's the bear Jo?' Christine asked. 'Where's the bear?'

Maman kept saying he was as pale as a ghost and should go and lie down. He appealed one last time to Grandpère, but Grandpère ruffled his hair proudly, took his hunting rifle from the corner of the room and went out with everyone else to hunt the bear.

'Was it big, Jo?' said Christine tugging at his arm.
She was full of questions. You could never ignore
Christine or her questions – she wouldn't let you.
'Was it as big as Hubert?' And she held up her
hands as high as she could.

'Bigger,' said Jo.

Bandaged like a wounded soldier he was taken up
to his bedroom and tucked under the blankets. He
stayed in bed only until Maman left the room, and
then he sprang out of bed and ran to the window.
He could see nothing but the narrow streets and the
grey roofs of the village, and beyond the church-
tower just a glimpse of the jagged mountain peaks
still white in places with winter snow. The streets
were empty of people, all except the priest, Father
Lasalle, who was hurrying past, his hand on his hat
to stop it blowing away.

All afternoon Jo watched as the clouds came
down and began to swallow the valley. It was just
after the church clock struck five that he heard a
distant baying of dogs, and shortly after a volley of
shots that echoed through the mountains and left a
terrible silence hanging over the village.

He was down in the Square half an hour later
with everyone else to watch the triumphant
procession as it wound its way through the streets.
Grandpère came first, Hubert gambolling alongside
him.

'We got her,' Grandpère was shouting. 'We got
her. Give us a hand here Hubert, give us a hand.'

And they disappeared together into the café. They brought out two chairs each and set them down in front of the war memorial.

Limp in death, carried on two long poles by four men, the bear rocked into view, blood on her lolling tongue. She was laid out on the chairs, her legs hanging down on either side, her snout pressed up against the back of a chair. Jo was looking everywhere for Rouf but could not find him. He asked Grandpère if he had seen him but like everyone else Grandpère was too busy telling the story of the hunt or having his photograph taken. It was the grocer, Armand Jollet, who took pride of place in the photograph; it seemed he was the one who had actually shot the bear. He proclaimed this noisily, his round face red with pride and exhilaration. 'Two hundred metres away I was, and I hit him right between the eyes.'

'It's a she,' said Father Lasalle bending over the bear.

'What's the difference?' said Armand Jollet. 'He or she, that skin's worth a fortune.'

In the celebrations that followed the photograph, the war was suddenly forgotten. Even Marie, Cousin Jean's young widow, was laughing with them, swept along on a tide of communal joy and relief. Hubert clapped and cavorted about the place like a wild thing. He reared up like a bear and roared around the streets chasing screaming children and shouting, 'Baar! Baar!' Jo looked down at the bear and stroked her back. The fur was long and close and soft, the body still warm with life. Blood from the bear's nose dropped on to his shoe and he felt suddenly sick. He turned to run away but Monsieur Sarthol had his arm around his shoulders and was calling for silence.

'Here's the lad himself,' he said. 'Without Jo Lalande there'd be no bear. This is the first bear we have shot in Lescun for over twenty-five years.'

'Thirty,' said Father Lasalle.

The Mayor ignored him and went on. 'Lord knows how many of our sheep she'd have killed. We've a lot to thank him for.' Jo saw Maman's eyes smiling back at him in the front of the crowd but he could not smile back. The Mayor lifted his glass – most people seemed to have a glass in their hand by now. 'So, here's to Jo and here's to the bear, and down with the Boche.'

'Long live the bear,' someone shouted and the laughter that followed echoed in Jo's head. He could stand it no longer. He pulled away and ran, ignoring Maman's call to come back.

Until the Mayor's speech he had not thought about his part in it all. The she-bear was lying there dead, spread out on the chairs in the Square and he knew now it was all his doing. And perhaps Rouf was out there in the hills with his throat torn out, and none of it would have happened if he had not fallen asleep.

He ran all the way back along the track to the sheep pastures and up towards the trees. He stood there and called for Rouf again and again until his voice cracked, but only the crows answered him. He pushed the tears back out of his eyes and tried to calm himself, to remember the exact spot where he'd last seen Rouf. He called again, he whistled; but the clouds seemed to soak up the echoes. He looked up. There were no longer any mountains to be seen above the tree line, only a pall of thick mist. It was still now, not a whisper of wind. He could see where the sheep had been; there was wool caught on the bark of the trees, there were droppings here, footprints there. And then he saw the blood, Rouf's blood perhaps, a brown smattering on the root of a tree.

He could not be sure what it was that he was hearing, not at first. He thought perhaps it was the mewing of an invisible buzzard flying through the clouds but then he heard the sound again and knew it for what it was, the whining of a dog — high-pitched and distant but now quite unmistakable. He called and he climbed, it was too steep to run. He ducked under low-slung branches, he clambered over fallen trees calling all the while: 'I'm coming Rouf, I'm coming.'

The whining was punctuated now with a strange, intermittent growling, quite unlike anything he had heard before. He came upon Rouf sooner than he had expected. He spotted him through the trees sitting still as a rock, his head lowered as if he was pointing. He did not even turn round to look as Jo broke through into the clearing behind him. He seemed intent upon something in the mouth of a small cave. It was brown and it was small; and then it moved and became a bear cub. It was sitting in the shadows and waving one of its front paws at Rouf. Jo crouched down and put a hand on Rouf's neck. Rouf looked up at him whining with excitement. He licked his lips and resumed his focus on the bear cub, his body taut. The bear cub rocked back against the side of the cave, legs apart, and growled. Yet it was hardly a growl, more a bleat of hunger, a cry for help, a call for mother. 'They'll kill him, Rouf,' he whispered. 'If they find out about him they'll hunt him down and kill him, just like his mother.' Still looking at the bear he stroked Rouf's neck. It was matted and wet to the touch – like blood – but when he looked down at Rouf there wasn't a mark on him.

Suddenly Rouf was on his feet, he swung round, hackles up, a rumbling growl in his throat. Jo turned. There was a man standing under the trees at the edge of the clearing. He wore a dirty black coat, a battered hat on his head. They looked at each other. Rouf stopped growling and his tail began to wag.

'Only me again,' said the man coming out of the trees towards them. Even with his hat he was a short man and as he came closer Jo saw that he had the gaunt, grey look of old men, yet his beard was rust red with not a fleck of white in it. There was a wine bottle in one hand and a stick in the other.

'Milk,' he said holding out the bottle. Rouf sniffed at it and the man laughed. 'Not for you,' he said and he patted Rouf on the head. 'For the little fellow. Starving he is. Perhaps you'd hold my stick for me,' he said. 'We don't want to frighten him do we?' He gave his hat to Jo as well and took off his coat. 'I saw the whole thing, you know. I saw you running off too. Your dog is he?' Jo nodded. 'Fights like a tiger doesn't he? Bears like that can knock your head off you know. One swipe of the paw that's all it takes. He was lucky. She tore his ear a bit, a lot of blood; but we soon cleaned you up didn't we old son? Right as rain he is now.' He bent down and poured some milk on to a rock. 'Now, let's see if we can get this little fellow to take a drink.' He backed away a few paces and knelt down. 'He'll smell it soon, you'll see. Give him time and he won't be able to resist it.' He sat back on his heels.

The cub ventured out of the shadows of the cave, lifting his nose and sniffing the air as he came. 'Come on, come on little fellow,' said the man, 'we won't hurt you.' And he reached out very slowly and poured out some more milk but closer to the bear cub this time. 'She could've got away you know.'

'Who?' said Jo.

'The bear, the mother bear. I've been thinking about it. She was leading them away from her cub. Deliberate it was, I'm sure of it. And what's more she led them a fair old dance I can tell you. Did you see the hunt?' Jo shook his head. 'Right away down the valley she took them, I saw it all – well most of

17

it anyway. Course I couldn't know why she was doing that, not at the time; and then I was on my way back home through the woods and there was this little fellow, and your dog just sitting here watching him. Covered in blood he was. Once I'd cleaned him up I went back home for some milk – the only thing I could think of. There you are, he's coming for it now.' The cub came forward tentatively, touched the milk with his paw, smelt it, licked it to taste and then began to lap noisily. Suddenly the man's free arm shot out and scooped the cub on to his lap. There was a flurry of paws and a furious scratching and yowling until all the flailing arms and legs were trapped. His whole head was white with milk by now but the end of the bottle was in his mouth and he was sucking in deeply. The man looked up at Jo and smiled. He had milk all over his beard and was licking his lips. 'Got him,' he said and he chuckled until he laughed. The cub still clung to the bottle when it was empty and would not let go.

'He'll die out here on his own won't he?' said Jo.

'No he won't, not if we don't let him,' said the man and he tickled the cub under his chin. 'Someone's going to have to look after him.'

'I can't,' said Jo. 'They'd kill him. If I took him home they'd kill him, I know they would.' He touched the pad of the cub's paw, it was harder than he'd expected. The man thought for a while nodding slowly.

'Well then, I'll have to do it, won't I?' he said.

'Won't be long, only a month or two at the most I should think and then he'll be able to cope on his own. I've got nothing much else to do with myself, not at the moment.' For just a moment as he caught his eye Jo thought he recognised the man from somewhere before but he could not think where. Yet he was sure he knew everyone who lived in the valley – not by name necessarily, but by place or by face. 'You don't know who I am do you?' said the man. It was as if he could read Jo's thoughts. Jo shook his head. 'Well that makes us even doesn't it, because I don't know you either. Maybe it's better it stays that way. You've got to promise me never to say a word, you understand?' There was a new urgency in his voice. 'There was no cub, you never met me, you never even saw me. None of this ever happened.' He reached out and gripped Jo's arm tightly. 'You have to promise me. Not a word to anyone – not your father, not your mother, not your best friend, no-one, not ever.'

'All right,' said Jo who was becoming alarmed. He felt the grip on his arm relax.

'Good boy, good boy,' he said and patted Jo's arm.

The man looked up. The mist was filtering down through the treetops above them. 'I'd better get back,' he said. 'I don't want to get caught out in this, I'll never find my way home.'

Once he was on his feet Jo gave him his hat and his stick. 'Now you hang on to that dog of yours,' he said. 'I don't want him following me home.

Where one goes others can follow, if you understand my meaning.' Jo wasn't sure he did. The cub clambered up his shoulder and put an arm around his neck. 'Seems to like me, doesn't he?' said the man. He turned to go and then stopped. 'And don't you go blaming yourself for what happened this afternoon. You had your job to do, and that old mother bear she had hers to do and that's all there is to it. Besides,' and he smiled broadly as the cub snuffled in his ear, 'besides, if none of it had happened, we'd never have met would we?'

'We haven't met,' said Jo catching Rouf by the scruff of his neck as he made to follow them. The man laughed.

'Nor we have,' he said. 'Nor we have. And if we haven't met we can't say goodbye can we?' And he turned, waved his stick above his head and walked away into the trees, the cub's chin resting on his shoulder. The eyes that looked back at Jo were two little moons of milk.

Chapter Two

Jo stood in the clearing and listened until he could no longer hear the man's footsteps. The whole day had been like a bad dream that had turned suddenly and intensely intriguing – a dream he wanted to cling to. He knew if he walked away now he might never see the man or the bear cub again. He had to find out who he was and where he was going. He knew he shouldn't but he had to follow him all the same.

Rouf did not have to be asked to follow the scent. He simply walked away into the trees and Jo went after him. From time to time he stopped to listen, but all he heard was Rouf's purposeful panting ahead of him and the soft whisper of the mist falling through the trees. After a while he began to wonder if Rouf's nose was failing him because they were following no track through the forest. Jo found himself sometimes climbing steeply and then scrambling downwards again clutching at treetrunks to keep himself upright. They seemed to be going back on themselves, almost round in circles at one point; but Rouf seemed sure enough of himself, plodding on resolutely until they broke out of the trees. Jo found himself looking down on the slate roofs of a farmstead.

He recognised at once where they were although he had never been near the place nor seen it from quite this direction. It was Widow Horcada's farm. She lived alone up in the hills and kept herself to herself. She seemed to like it that way. She must have had a husband once but Jo had never known him and no-one ever spoke of him. So far as anyone could tell she lived off her pigs that wandered everywhere – much to everyone's annoyance – off one cow and off her honey; you could find her beehives ranged all along the hillside above the village. There was a line of them below him now, just a few metres away, but no bees that Jo could see. Jo had no desire to go any closer, and it wasn't because he was afraid of bees.

Widow Horcada was not much liked in the village – 'sinister' Maman always called her – although Grandpère always defended her stoutly. The children in the village called her 'The Black Widow', and not just on account of the long black shawl she always wore over her head. Like every child in the village Jo had been mauled more than once by her sharp tongue. She made no secret of the fact that she did not like children, boys in particular. She was a person to avoid. He would go no further. But before Jo could grab him, Rouf was making his way past the beehives and down towards the buildings. Jo followed, whispering as loud as he dared for Rouf to stop. But Rouf did not stop.

There was a cow grazing in the small paddock below the house, her bell sounded as she pulled at the grass and looked up. The walled farmyard was full of snuffling, snorting pigs and that was clearly too much for Rouf – he did not like pigs, not one bit. He sat down outside the wall and waited for Jo. A light was on in the house and there were dark figures moving about in the downstairs room. There were voices coming from inside, raised voices; but he was too far away to hear what they were saying. One thing was certain though; one of the voices belonged to the man he had been following.

Jo thought of jumping the wall and running low across the yard towards the window but the boar was wandering towards him with menace in his eyes; so Jo went around the back. There was only one window, and to reach it he would have to climb up a stack of wood that was piled high against the wall. He climbed carefully until he could pull himself up and peer over the windowsill.

There were two people in the room. The man was bent over the sink splashing water over his face and Widow Horcada sat in a chair by the stove knitting feverishly. She was shaking her head and muttering something that Jo couldn't hear. The man was wiping his face with a towel and talking through it at the same time.

'Don't you go worrying yourself about the boy,' he said. 'He doesn't know who I am, what I am or where I live. We'll be all right.' He dropped the towel over the back of a chair and sat down at the table feeling his beard. 'Worst thing about a beard,' he said, 'it never dries properly.' And at that moment Jo remembered where he'd seen the man before.

It was the last summer before Papa had gone off to the war and he'd been up in the high mountain pastures with Papa, the first time he'd been allowed to go. Three long months they had spent up there together in the hut, milking the sheep every morning, making the cheese, then milking the sheep again in the evening. It had been a summer of hard work and soaring happiness – a summer alone with Papa, a summer living close to the eagles. Most people walking in the mountains passed by with a 'Good morning', or perhaps a request to drink at the spring but only two had ever come into the hut. They had appeared early one morning, a man with a red beard, a little girl clutching his hand. She'd have been five or six years old maybe with red hair like his. They had stayed until noon watching the sheep being milked and the cheese being made. They sat side by side and silent on Papa's bed and watched fascinated as the rennet was poured in, as they heated and stirred the milk in the cauldrons, as

Papa gathered the curd in his hands and squeezed out the whey. Jo remembered their silence and the intense seriousness on the little girl's face. They asked the way up to the Spanish border and went off. It was raining when they came back later that afternoon. They brought with them a bunch of flowers, pinks they were and wild pansies. Jo could see them now in her hand. 'From Spain to you,' said the little girl, ushered forward by her father; and the man with the beard told them how they had walked to the top of the mountain and looked into Spain and how their legs ached. Papa had given them towels to dry themselves off. 'Never grow a beard young man,' the man had told him as he wiped his face. 'You can never get it dry.' Jo remembered Papa thanking them rather awkwardly and saying that no-one had ever given him flowers before. They were already leaving before they introduced themselves. 'I'm Madame Horcada's son-in-law,' he said shaking Papa's hand, 'and this is my daughter, Anya.'

Watching them walk away down the mountain Papa had told him the story of Widow Horcada's daughter – Florence she was called. Jo thought he remembered seeing her in church once when he was little but he couldn't be sure. She'd gone off to Paris Papa told him, run off some said, and got herself married. No-one knew who to because she'd never brought him back to Lescun. 'So that was the husband,' said Papa. 'Well I never.'

'Where's Widow Horcada's daughter?' Jo had

asked.

'Dead,' said Papa. 'Dead in childbirth I heard, and that must be the child. Poor little mite.' Papa had kept the dead flowers all summer long on the shelf above his bed but they never spoke of the visitors again.

'Foolhardy,' said Widow Horcada, putting the knitting down on her lap. 'Plain foolhardy, that's what it was. I just don't understand what came over you, Benjamin. Stay as long as it takes I said. Do what you have to do and I'll help you all I can. We agreed, didn't we? You promised you'd go out only at night. You promised me, didn't you? And what do you do? You go out for a walk in broad daylight. A walk! And what do you bring back? Not berries, not herbs, not mushrooms, but an orphan bear cub. I ask you Benjamin, haven't we got troubles enough?' She leaned forward in her chair, her crooked finger pointing. 'And that boy you met, what happens now, eh? You tell me that. What happens when he runs home and tells them all down in the village? Well, I'll tell you. Someone will put two and two together and they'll know the old widow's son-in-law is back. They don't forget a face you know, especially not your face. They may be country folk, Benjamin, but they're not stupid.'

The man left the table and crouched down in front of her taking both her hands in his. 'Believe me, Grandmère,' he said, 'the boy won't say anything. I can always tell an honest face.' He smiled up at her. 'I know I'm not all you wanted in a son-in-law but I tell you true, you're all I could ever have wanted in a mother-in-law.'

'Go on with you,' she said trying to push him away, but he held on to her hands.

'No I mean it. You're brave and you're good and I couldn't have done any of it without you. You know that.'

'I don't know anything,' she said, 'not any more I don't. Maybe you're right about that boy, maybe he won't say anything. Let's just pray to God you're right.'

'Your God or mine?' said the man laughing.

'Why not both?' the widow said, 'just in case one of us is barking up the wrong tree.' She reached out and touched his face. 'You're all I've got left now Benjamin, you and little Anya – if she's still alive.'

'Course she is,' said the man. 'How many times do I have to tell you?'

'You've been telling me for two years now,' said the widow.

'Two years, ten years,' he said, 'however long it takes. She'll come. And when she does we'll be waiting for her just like I promised her. She knows where to come and she'll be here, you'll see. She could walk in here tonight.'

Widow Horcada sighed and looked up at the window. 'It's getting dark,' she said, starting up from her chair, 'I'd better see to the animals.' And then she saw him.

Jo felt the logs give under his feet. He tried to hold on to the window ledge but his fingers were cold and would not grip as they should. For a fleeting moment he saw their faces staring up at him and then he was falling in an avalanche of logs that sent him tumbling down on to the cobbled stone of the yard. He kicked frantically and pushed the logs away. Then he was on his feet and running before he heard the back door open. He dared not turn round and look. For the second time that day Jo found himself running down the slopes, but this time there was a misty darkness to hide him and he could afford to stop from time to time to regain his breath. Rouf ran on ahead of him and was waiting for him on his sack by the front doorstep. Jo had to step over him to open the door. Rouf yawned hugely and put his head on his paws. Clearly for him it had been no more than an ordinary day.

* * *

For some weeks after this the village was diverted, its spirits lifted by stories of the great bear hunt, stories that eclipsed even the grim news of the war, of more German victories everywhere. They heard about the world outside through newspapers that few people believed because they were controlled by the Germans, but also through Radio London and what you heard there had to be believed. There was no consolation to be gleaned from either source, so they talked of the bear hunt to forget the war and for a time they could do so.

At school Jo had become quite the hero and that was not entirely to his liking. If Jo had learned one lesson at school it was that it was better to keep a low profile – that way you kept out of trouble. But now he was thrust suddenly into the limelight. He had admirers and therefore enemies too. Even his best friend, Laurent, seemed to look at him differently. Only Monsieur Audap, his teacher, was quite unimpressed by the whole thing. Strict as he was, severe even at times, Monsieur Audap was scrupulously fair, and was liked and respected for it. A retiring man, he said very little, but what he did say was always worth listening to.

The day after Armand Jollet put up the bearskin on the wall of his grocer's shop for all the world to admire, Monsieur Audap spent the entire morning telling the children all about the mountain bears, about where they lived and how they lived. After hibernation, he said, in the Spring when their body fat was low and they had young to feed, then they would dare anything to find food enough to provide for themselves and for their cubs. Bears, he said, never came close to people unless they had to. They knew of their cruelty, of their voracious appetite for killing and of their greed. Bears, he said, were neither stupid nor suicidal. This one must have been starving to have risked such an attack. Almost certainly, said Monsieur Audap, she had cubs to feed – usually there were two, maybe just one. They'd be dead by now, of course. They needed their mother's milk for at least three or four months. Jo looked down at his desk so that his eyes would not betray him.

As time passed though the bear talk both in and out of school became less frequent and less triumphalist; and once again news of the war, of unending, depressing defeats began to preoccupy the village. But to many of the children, to Jo too, the war was still an unreal thing. In over two years of war they had not seen a single German soldier, no planes, no tanks, nothing. The war was in the talk and they heard plenty of that; and talk almost always meant argument. What should they do? Should they save what could be saved? Should they accept the finality of defeat and join Maréchal Pétain, or should they fight on with the English and join the French colonel, whose name Jo could never remember but who had broadcast from London that the war was not over, that the Germans could be beaten, must be beaten and would be beaten? And all the while they waited for the prisoners-of-war to come home and they didn't. They waited for the Germans to come and they didn't.

'I just want it over with, Jo,' Maman said. 'I want your father home. I don't care what it takes. I want it like it was before.' And although Grandpère did not often argue with her openly, Jo knew what he thought. 'That Colonel in London, that De Gaulle, he's our only hope I tell you,' Grandpère had told him. 'Him and the English. I don't like the English, never have done, but at least they're fighting the Germans and anyone who is fighting them is a friend of France, that's how I see it. And I should know, Jo, I fought them before, remember? We beat them then and we'll beat them again. We've got to. There'll be nothing left for you or for any of us if we don't.' What Jo thought about the war and about the Occupation seemed to depend on whether he had just talked to Maman or to Grandpère: he could never make up his mind.

Jo thought often of Papa as he sat on his rock watching the sheep. He had missed him at first, the loudness of him about the house and the smell of him when he came in from work; but now as time passed he was enjoying his new role as the man about the house. He enjoyed sitting in Papa's chair at the kitchen table and doing Papa's work about the farm. But whether it was the war or whether it was Papa competing for his thoughts, Jo's mind was always drawn back to the bear cub and the man he'd met in the woods on the day of the bear hunt. He had to know who he was, what he was hiding from and why he was waiting for Anya. Every passing day only intensified his longing to go back up to the Widow Horcada's farm to find out what was going on and to see the bear cub again. But there was always work to be done, farm work, school work. It was difficult to get away – that was what he told himself anyway.

Grandpère took the sheep to the high pastures that summer. Jo was still too young, Maman said, to do it on his own and she didn't want him missing any more school. 'You only get your learning once,' she said, and besides she needed him at home – there was the bracken to cut and to turn, or the hay to make; and at weekends there were the supplies to be taken up to Grandpère in the mountains and the cheeses brought back to be salted, stored and sold. The work was long and hard, but if Jo was honest with himself – and as time passed he had to be – he knew the work was an excuse. The fact was that he could not summon up the courage to go back to Widow Horcada's farm. Every time he had seen her coming he'd hidden from her; and the one time he couldn't avoid her, when she'd come into the grocer's shop, he'd run out without buying what he went in there for. He hadn't even dared to look her in the eye to see if she recognised him as the boy peering in through her window that evening.

Time and again he had looked up the hillside towards her farmhouse and had seen the Widow Horcada out in her fields, making her hay, milking her cow or driving her pigs, but there'd been no sign of anyone else. He was beginning to think he had imagined the whole thing.

Then one blustery Autumn day, after the sheep had come down from the pastures and he was spreading out the bracken for their bedding in the barn, he saw Widow Horcada scurrying past, black scarf over her head, flowers in her hand. He knew she'd be making for the churchyard to put flowers on her husband's grave. She'd stop to do her shopping on the way back, she always did. Jo knew he had a clear half hour to get up there and back: he could do it if he hurried. She'd never see him, not if he was careful. Rouf tried to come with him as he always did. He shut him in the barn and shouted to Maman that he wouldn't be long.

He kept under the cover of the trees as long as he could. From there he could see without being seen. Her pigs were foraging in the field below the house and the cow was lying curled asleep in the middle of them. There was no-one about. He threw caution to the wind because he had to – there was no time for anything else. He hared across the field until he reached the safety of the barn wall where he knew he could not be seen from the house. He ran around the back of the barn and into the courtyard behind. There was no sound except for the contented grunting of rooting pigs. He was creeping past the barn door when he heard something shuffling around inside. The bear cub, it must be the bear cub.

He looked about him and then opened the door slowly. Like all the barns it was long and low and dark, with bracken on the floor and hay in the wooden rack that ran the length of the wall. But there was no bear cub, and no other animals either. Yet he was sure he'd heard something, quite sure. He pushed the door wide open so as to throw as much light as possible down the barn. There was one small dirty window at the far end, and the shutters were banging open and shut, first one and then the other. Jo peered into the darkness. He would go no further. He could see well enough from the doorway. He was turning to go when he

33

trod on something. He bent down and picked up a shoe, a child's shoe. The strap was broken. He thought little of it at first. He would have dropped it and left had he not heard the breathing – a regular wheezing breathing.

It came quite definitely from the hayrack about half-way down the barn. Jo took a few steps towards it and the breathing stopped. He thought of the bear cub and of the hibernation Monsieur Audap had told them about, but he thought that it couldn't be the bear cub because it wasn't winter yet and anyway a bear cub would hardly be sleeping in a hayrack – but then perhaps it would. He took a few more tentative steps forward and peered into the hay. The breathing began again a little further on and quite suddenly he found himself not looking at hay at all but at two eyes that stared back at him unblinking and terrified. Jo could do nothing for a moment but stare back into them. They were not the eyes of a bear for the face that went with them was pale and thin under a fringe of dark hair.

Jo backed away slowly, swallowing his fear. He had the presence of mind to close the door quietly and it was just as well he did for across the yard Widow Horcada was bent over, holding a bucket under an outdoor tap. She had her back to him and was humming quietly to herself. For a few moments he stood looking at her disbelieving. How could she be back so soon? It wasn't possible. Yet there she was in front of him. She had only to turn round. It was just a few steps to the corner of the barn and safety. He'd make it if he could move silently. Without taking his eyes off her he began to inch his way along the wall.

He knew he should have looked where he was going. He told himself so as the fork he blundered into clattered to the ground. Jo looked at the Widow Horcada, the bucket fell out of her hand as the black shawl swung round. Jo dropped the shoe, stumbled over the fork and ran and ran. He rounded the corner of the barn, but there he was stopped in his tracks, for up the hill, a large basket in one hand, a stick in the other, came Widow Horcada. She looked up, saw him and shouted at him. He could not hear what she was saying. Jo turned again and ran back into the yard – it was the only way he could go. She was there too and coming towards him. He looked now from one to the other. Fear crept up his spine like a warm cat and he felt the hair rise on the back of his neck. Never in all his life had he felt like screaming until this moment. He wanted to but he could not. And then one of them spoke, the one striding across the yard towards him.

'It's me.' It was a man's voice. 'It's me.' And he pulled the shawl off his head. The red beard was longer than Jo remembered but it was the same man. 'Don't you remember me?' he said.

Chapter Three

Jo had nowhere to run to even if he'd wanted to and he wasn't sure now that he did. The man stooped to pick up the shoe.

'And where did you find this then?' he asked.

'In the barn,' said Jo. 'I was only looking. I thought you might have the bear cub in there.' The man wiped the shoe on the end of the shawl. There were footsteps coming into the yard behind him. Jo turned. The Black Widow stood there breathing hard, resting her weight on her stick. The man went over to her and took the basket.

'It's all right Grandmère,' he said putting an arm around her. 'It's that boy, the same boy.' Widow Horcada limped across the yard towards him. It was all Jo could do not to back away. She looked at him long and hard.

'Well, well,' she said, 'so it was you. I thought as much. I wasn't sure, not until you pushed past me in the shop the other day. I knew then all right. You shouldn't go peeking through other people's windows.' She caught sight of the shoe in the man's hand. 'So he knows then,' she said.

'He's been in the barn,' he said.

'Has he indeed?' said the Widow. 'And what did you find in there boy?'

There was no point in futile protestations and denials but Jo tried them anyway. 'I don't know what you mean,' he said feebly.

She stabbed her stick into the ground by his foot. 'Besides the shoe,' she said, 'did you see anything else in there? Well, did you?' Jo looked down to avoid her eyes. 'I don't like a child that won't look me in the eye,' she said and she lifted his chin until he had to look at her. Jo had never looked at her this closely and he was surprised by what he saw. It was not the cruel face he had always supposed but leathery and lined with age and work.

'Yes, I did,' Jo said. She released his chin.

'And do you always speak the truth?' she asked quietly.

Jo shook his head. 'No,' he said and her face cracked into a sudden smile.

'Seems you were right then, Benjamin. A rare thing, an honest boy. Inside,' she said, 'bring him inside,' and she walked away towards the door. 'Boys like honey,' she said. 'We'll give him some honey.' And she disappeared inside the house.

Jo was reluctant to follow. The man put a hand on his shoulder. 'Have you still got him?' Jo asked.

'The bear cub, have you still got him?'

The man shook his head. 'Not any more. A month after we found him, just as soon as I thought he could fend for himself, I took him high up into the mountains and left him but he's been coming back from time to time. I think maybe he thinks of me as his mother, either that or he just doesn't like being on his own. Come on.'

Widow Horcada was putting a plate of honeycomb out on the table. Suddenly the old lady leaned forward and had to hold on to the table to steady herself. The man was by her side at once and helped her to her chair.

'You've been overdoing it again,' he said. 'I've told you haven't I?'

'Don't fuss,' she said, pushing him away. 'Don't fuss me. I'll be all right. Sit down boy, sit down over there in the light, I want to be able to see your face.' Jo sat down at the table. 'Eat up, boy, eat up.' She had a strange habit of wrinkling her nose and sniffing and Jo found it difficult not to stare at her. He cut out a corner of the honeycomb and spread it on the bread. The man was hanging the big shawl on the back of the door.

'I know your father,' said Widow Horcada, not taking her eyes off his face. 'Prisoner-of-war isn't he?' Jo nodded. 'I knew your grandfather better though. I told you about him didn't I Benjamin?' Benjamin nodded and she turned back to Jo. 'I nearly married him once. Did he ever tell you that, boy? Sweethearts we were.' She sighed and sat back in her chair. 'Ah well, we both went our separate ways for better or for worse. You're not eating, boy.' Jo took another mouthful. 'Jo Lalande he's called, aren't you, boy? And you know who I am don't you?' Jo nodded. 'This is Benjamin, my son-in-law, but then of course you've met him before, haven't you?' She paused for a moment, her searching eyes still fixed on Jo. She blew her nose and tucked her handkerchief into her sleeve. 'Well,' she said. 'I suppose he'll have to be told. Nothing else for it is there? But I don't like it. I don't like it one bit.'

'It'll be all right,' said Benjamin. He was standing behind her now and looking down at Jo. 'What he doesn't know already – and he knows plenty – he's guessed at, and guessing is a lot more dangerous than knowing. And we know we can trust him. After all he's known about us for months now, and he's not said a word. If he had then we'd have known about it you can be sure of that. We'd have had the police knocking on the door in the middle of the night by now. No, we don't need to worry about him. We can trust him.'

'Let's hope so,' said the Widow wearily. 'Let's hope so.'

Benjamin came and sat down opposite Jo at the table. 'It's difficult to know where to start, Jo,' he said, 'but since I'm the cause of all the trouble I'll start with me. I'm a Jew,' he said. 'D'you know what that is?'

'They're in the Bible aren't they?' said Jo.

Benjamin shook his head and laughed. 'Yes,' he said. 'We're in the Bible and there's plenty of people think that's where we should've stayed.' He looked down at his hands and picked at the corner of his thumb nail. 'It was all rumours at first,' he went on, 'rumours you couldn't believe, rumours you didn't want to believe. But bit by bit the rumours became facts, facts that had to be believed. They began on their own Jews, in Germany. First they took away their work, then their property; and they made them wear yellow stars on their coats. Then they started rounding them up and sending them off to the camps. We knew it was happening but we thought we were safe enough in Paris, me and little Anya – Anya, she's my daughter. But of course we weren't. They invaded France and Paris fell. There was only one place left we could go. We came here for a holiday a few years back, Anya and me, to see where her mother was brought up, to see Grandmère. The happiest time of our lives it was too. So when the invasion came we decided to come back here.'

'Best place too, long as you're sensible,' said the Widow Horcada pointedly. 'Safe as houses and you can be over the border in five hours.'

'I walked it once,' said Benjamin, 'with Anya.'

'I know,' said Jo. 'You picked flowers for my father.'

Benjamin frowned for a moment and then his eyes brightened suddenly. 'So it was you. You were the boy. You remember I told you, Grandmère, that day that we watched the shepherd making cheese. He was your father?' Jo nodded. 'And you were the little boy, weren't you? Well, well, it's a small world.' The light left his eyes as quickly as it had come. 'We left Paris together, Anya and me. Trouble was everyone was doing the same thing and the roads were jammed with cars and carts and lorries and people – thousands of people, everyone trying to get away. They machine-gunned us from the air whenever they felt like it and when the planes came we all scattered. After they'd gone it was always difficult to find each other again; so we made an agreement, Anya and me, that if we were separated we would find our way back here, to Grandmère's house at Lescun, we would wait for each other and then we could escape together into Spain. We said we'd wait, we promised each other.' His voice choked, and it was a moment or two before he went on. 'And that's just how it happened. One evening – just outside Poitiers it was – the planes came and strafed us and we all ran for shelter into the forest. When they'd gone I looked everywhere for her. All night I looked for her, all next day and the day after, but I couldn't find her. So that's why I'm here and that's why I'll be staying till Anya comes.'

'But what about her, in there,' said Jo, 'in the barn?'

'She's called Léah,' said Benjamin. 'Same age to the month as Anya. She comes from Poland just like my family did many years ago. We've got two

41

more coming soon.'

'Two more?'

'Children,' said Widow Horcada sniffing. 'Jewish children. He collects them, don't you Benjamin?' Benjamin said nothing. 'They get passed down all through France and when they get here he keeps them for a week maybe, sometimes longer, till they're strong enough for the journey; and then he takes them over the mountains into Spain and to safety.'

'And so many of them,' said Benjamin, 'so many are just like Léah. She had a big family, eight children there were. She's the oldest and she's the last. She was lucky; she was out when the soldiers came to the house. She watched her family being taken away, and she's been on the run ever since. But she got here, and that's why we'll never give up hope. If Léah can get here all the way from Poland then so can Anya. One day Anya will be one of these children and we'll be waiting for her.'

'That shawl you were wearing,' said Jo.

Ben was smiling again. 'Oh that. That was your idea, wasn't it Grandmère? Do you know, Jo, I never once went out of this house for two years unless it was to take the children over the mountains and then it was always in the dark. Then the first time I venture out for a walk in the daytime I bump into you, and I bring home a bear cub. She wasn't too pleased about that. She lets me out by day now, but only if I stay close to the house and only if I dress up to look like her. She's a terrible tyrant is my mother-in-law.'

'Stuff and nonsense,' she said.

At that moment they all heard something at the door. They saw the handle turn. It opened slowly, squeaking on its hinges, and a small face peered round. It was the girl from the barn. Benjamin ran across the room and pulled her inside. Then he looked out of the door and shut it, leaning back against it and breathing hard. 'It's all right,' he said. When he spoke again it was in a language Jo could not understand. He crouched down, holding the girl by her shoulders, and he was clearly angry with her. But the girl was not listening to him. Her eyes were fixed on the honey on the table beside Jo. She walked towards it now as if she was in a trance. She pulled the plate towards her, dug her finger into the honeycomb and scooped it into her mouth.

'She eats all the time,' said Widow Horcada. 'It's like she's never eaten before.'

The girl saw her shoe on the table and took it. She dropped it on to the floor and stepped into it without looking down. Jo looked at her as she ate. Her face was impassive except for her eyes that flitted nervously around the room. There was hay in her hair and on her coat. Benjamin beckoned her over and she went slowly towards him. When she sat on his lap she looked back at Jo, sucking her finger. And then Benjamin began to sing softly in the girl's ear. She put her hand up and curled her fingers in his beard. It was a song Jo had never heard before and in a strange language. He sang in a deep resonant voice that filled the room. He rocked her back and forth as he sang and gradually she settled back against his shoulder and hummed with him. All the while she never stopped looking at Jo. She was asleep in a few minutes, her finger in her mouth.

'I've told you Benjamin, I've told you,' Widow Horcada was whispering, 'they must stay in the barn. You must tell her, Benjamin. We can't have them wandering around. They must stay where they're told.'

'You're right,' said Benjamin, 'but I have told her, again and again. She's lonely in there, Grandmère. When the others come it'll be better. She'll have friends then and she'll stay put.'

'All right,' said the Widow. 'But just you make sure she does. Just a glimpse of one of those children of yours and we're done for – you know that don't you?'

'I know,' said Benjamin. 'I know.'

She turned to Jo. 'And you'd best be off home.' As Jo got up she reached out and grabbed his wrist. 'I was thinking,' she said, drawing him towards her. 'I was thinking of swearing you to secrecy.' She patted a book on the table beside her. 'On the Bible. Do I need to?'

'No,' said Jo.

'Off you go then,' said Widow Horcada, 'and if you see me down in the village behave like they all do, all except Hubert. He's the only one that smiles at me, but then he smiles at everyone doesn't he?

Don't even look at me. I'm still the Black Widow, remember?' Jo turned to go. 'And another thing, boy; stay away from here. Don't come back. We don't want any comings and goings. I want them to forget I'm here. It's safer that way. You understand?'

'Yes,' said Jo.

She waved him away. 'Off home with you now.'

Jo was so occupied with his thoughts as he made his way home that he took no notice at all of the empty, silent streets; but as he reached the Square his thoughts were rudely interrupted. The whole village was there standing hushed and unmoving, like mourners at a funeral. Jo eased his way through the crowd so that he could see what was going on. An armoured truck stood in the centre of the Square with four soldiers in black uniforms and shining helmets sitting erect in the back of it. Beside it Monsieur Sarthol was talking earnestly to a tall German officer who appeared not to be listening. 'Ja, ja,' he said dismissively. 'Ja, ja,' and he turned to the soldier beside him and nodded. The soldier walked towards the Mairie, the crowd parting in front of him. He leaned his rifle against the wall and pinned up a poster. Jo could see two faces on it and some writing below. The officer clicked his heels, saluted the Mayor and got back into the truck.

Hubert was standing next to Grandpère, towering over him. There was naked anger on his face. Jo knew he was going to do something; he could feel it coming. He did not have long to wait.

45

Hubert barged his way through the crowd and walked straight towards the German officer. He was carrying a short stick in his hand. The soldier walking back from the Mairie, saw Hubert and readied his rifle. The officer shouted to him and held up his hand. Hubert kept walking until he was about a metre away from the officer. Slowly and deliberately he raised his stick to his shoulder and pointed it at his face. 'Bang,' he said softly. 'Bang, bang, bang.' The mayor was rushing forward. He grabbed Hubert by the arm and pulled him back.

'He's my son,' he said. 'He doesn't mean anything. It's just his little joke. He's not quite right in the head, you understand. A bit simple. He won't hurt you.' The officer nodded curtly and motioned the soldier to get in.

Throughout this the four soldiers in the truck had sat impassive, their rifles between their knees. Jo stared at them and despite himself he could not but admire them. They were undeniably splendid in their immaculate uniforms. These were the black knights who had conquered wherever they went. He was staring at one of them in particular when the helmet turned, glinting in the sun, and Jo found his gaze suddenly returned. The eyes that held his were blue and cold and they chilled Jo to the heart. He looked away quickly. The truck started up, circled the Square and was gone.

Everyone crowded towards the poster, but Monsieur Sarthol stepped in front of it and held up his hand.

'All in good time,' he shouted. 'All in good time. First you must hear what he told me.' People still weren't listening and he raised his voice. 'You've got to listen to me. You've got to hear it.' They quietened enough for him to go on. 'He came to remind us that all of France is now occupied, that we are in a forbidden zone, that no-one goes in or out without the proper papers.'

'As if we didn't know that,' shouted Grandpère, and others shouted with him.

Monsieur Sarthol held up his hands. 'There's more,' he said. 'There's more. I had him with me for half an hour inside the Mairie, and there's a lot more.' Hubert was picking the bark off his stick. 'He came to inform us that they are going to garrison Lescun. Within days there'll be a company of soldiers living here.' He went on over the hubbub. 'And from tonight onwards, he said, there's going to be round the clock patrols along the border – hundreds of soldiers posted all along the frontier. He made it quite plain to me that from now on no-one would ever be able to escape into Spain. And he made it quite plain too that anyone helping fugitives will be shot.' The crowd was suddenly quiet. 'He means it. I'm telling you he means it. That poster there says he means it. Frenchmen, Jews, escaping prisoners-of-war, anyone – if you help them and you're caught you will be shot.' He stepped aside and pointed at the poster behind him. 'Just like those two. From Bedous they were. Patric Léon and André Latour. I

knew André, I knew him well, and so did most of
you. They shot them last week. They were caught
taking a family of Jews over the mountains into
Spain.'

The crowd turned away, some crossing
themselves, some murmuring prayers. Jo walked
over to the poster and looked into the faces of the
two men. They stared back at him, living eyes that
were now dead. Hubert was beside him and he was
crying. It was only at that moment that Jo realised
that the war had come at last to Lescun, to his
valley. Now and for the first time he understood the
terrible danger that faced Widow Horcada and
Benjamin if they were ever caught. Suddenly it was
all real. This was the enemy his father had fought
against. This was what happened when you lost a
war and the enemy occupied your country.

He thought at once of going straight back up to
Widow Horcada's house to warn them about the
patrols on the border, to tell them about what had
happened to the two men from Bedous, but he
decided there was no immediate danger. After all
the Germans had left the village, and besides he
remembered the Widow saying that the children
always rested up for a few days before Benjamin
took them over the mountains. There was no hurry.
Jo walked away from the poster and when he
looked back into the Square Hubert was still
standing there beside Monsieur Sarthol and Father
Lasalle who were talking together. Suddenly
Hubert lifted his stick, put it to his shoulder and

pointed it down the road in the direction the armoured truck had taken. 'Bang!' he shouted. 'Bang! Bang! Bang! Bang!' Monsieur Sarthol swung round, pulled the stick out of his hand and broke it over his knee. Hubert hung his head and walked away.

'That Hubert,' said Maman that evening, 'he could have got himself killed.'

They were salting the cheeses, a job that Jo hated. The salt always found out a nick or a scratch in his hand and stung him.

'Maybe,' said Grandpère. 'Maybe. But he was just doing what all of us wanted to do if only we'd had the courage to do it.'

'And what good would that do?' said Maman. 'Tell me that. You shoot one of them and they shoot twenty of us. Haven't you heard what they've done?'

'There's always a price to be paid,' said Grandpère, wiping his hands with a cloth, 'and anyway you can't believe everything you hear. Those poor boys,' he went on, 'those poor, brave boys.'

'Brave and dead,' said Maman.

'Well, maybe it's better that way,' he said.

Jo had been thinking of other things. 'What's a Jew?' he asked.

'What?' said Maman.

'A Jew. Those two men who were shot. They were taking some Jews into Spain. That's what Monsieur Sarthol said.'

Grandpère and Maman looked at each other. For several moments neither seemed to know what to say.

'Well,' said Grandpère at last. 'It's difficult to say exactly what he is, your Jew. He's not a Christian that's for sure, and he's not a Catholic. He's not like you and me. Doesn't go to church.'

'They haven't got churches,' said Maman, 'they've got temples haven't they? In the Bible they've got temples. Solomon was a Jew, and David – all those people.'

'But why do the Germans want them?' said Jo. 'What did they do?'

Grandpère thought for a moment. 'Well,' he said. 'Hard to say. Hard to say. The Germans, they don't need much excuse do they? What they don't like they kill, and what they want they take. They don't need reasons, and even if they do they invent them as they go along.'

Christine shouted from upstairs, loudly and urgently. 'Oh that child. She'll drive me mad,' said Maman, blowing her hair back out of her eyes as she lifted another cheese on to the shelf. 'She's on the go from the minute she wakes up. Can I ride Rouf? Can I ride the donkey? Play with me, Maman. Play with me, Maman.' She sighed deeply. 'Jo, be a dear and see to her for me will you? We'll finish off here.' And she went on as Jo went out: 'Those soldiers today, they were so young.'

'They're old enough,' said Grandpère. 'Quite old enough.'

Jo lay awake for most of that night. Neither the wind that rattled the shutters, nor Christine's crying, nor his racing thoughts would let him sleep; and when he did drop off into a doze he was soon trying to extricate himself from a hideous, recurring dream. A rearing bear was chasing him remorselessly through the forest, through trees that seemed to clutch at him and tear at his clothes, trees that turned into black helmetted soldiers who caught him by the arms and held him fast and then stood him against a wall to be shot. Each time he managed to drag himself out of the dream just before they shot him and each time he determined to stay awake till dawn; but dawn was a long time coming that night. As he lay in the dark he began to worry that he should have warned Widow Horcada and Benjamin at once about the patrols on the border. He'd have to tell them just as soon as he could.

It was difficult to find time to get away without being missed. He was kept busy with sheep all morning, but at midday Grandpère left him alone with them on the hillside. 'Don't you go dropping off,' Grandpère said and he was gone. Sometimes Jo thought that Grandpère had guessed what had happened that day when the bear came. That wasn't the first time he'd hinted at it. He sat for some time on the rock and scanned the hills around him. His eyes came to rest on Widow Horcada's farm high above him. A vulture circled over the house and he watched it floating away over the trees beyond. He saw a shawl-wrapped figure come out of the door and cross the yard and he wondered which of them it was. He had to find a way to tell them but he could not leave the sheep. Had Hubert not come whistling by in mid-afternoon he would never have been able to leave them. Hubert was everyone's spare shepherd, particularly theirs, and he was good at it too. 'I'll only be half an hour or so,' said Jo, as Hubert settled down on the rock fixing his eyes on the sheep. He always took his job very seriously. Jo knew he would not move until he got back. He left him there grunting meaningfully at Rouf, who looked up at him with perfect understanding in his eyes.

Jo kept to the trees for as long as he could and then dashed out across the field towards the house. Widow Horcada was waiting for him in the yard leaning on her stick. She seemed surprised, even annoyed to see him.

'You,' she said. 'I thought I told you to stay away.'

'I had to come,' said Jo. 'I had to tell you.'

'Tell me what?' said Widow Horcada.

'The Germans, they were in the village yesterday. There's hundreds of them all along the frontier. I had to warn you.' Widow Horcada's eyes were suddenly wide with anxiety. 'And they've shot people too,' said Jo. 'Two of them from Bedous. They were helping Jews to escape over the mountains like Benjamin does.' He looked around. 'Where is Benjamin?'

'Gone,' said Widow Horcada. 'He saw the soldiers down another road. He went last night with Léah. He wouldn't wait. He thought they'd come searching the houses. I told him not to go, but he wouldn't listen. He wouldn't wait.' She looked up towards the mountains. 'Something's wrong, I know it is. He should be back by now. He should be back.'

Chapter Four

Someone had to go and find out what had happened to them and Jo knew it would have to be him. There was no-one else who could go. It was too far and too steep for Widow Horcada.

'Which way does he go?' Jo asked. 'The Col de Loraille?'

'Usually,' she said.

There were only a few hours of light left, he'd have to hurry. As he turned to go Widow Horcada caught him by the arm.

'You take care now, boy, d'you hear me?'

'Course,' he said and he was out of the door and running.

From the field below the house he could see Hubert squatting on the rock, a hand on Rouf's neck. The sheep were spread out around him, yellow in the afternoon sun. Come the evening Hubert would drive the sheep home with Rouf. Jo

had often gone off eagle watching and left Hubert
to bring them in — he'd know what to do. Jo
reached the trees and made his way through them
down towards the river. From there on he'd be
climbing all the way. He knew the path to the Col
de Loraille well. It was the route up to their high
summer pastures, to Papa's hut. The trees were loud
with wind and the leaves were falling all about him.
He followed the tumbling river upwards. Ahead of
him, when the trees allowed, he could see the circle
of sharp peaks at the head of the valley and above
him the clouds raced each other back towards
Lescun. He thought of shouting for them but he
knew it would be pointless. Nothing could be heard
over the roar of the river and the gusting wind.
Every now and then he'd stop to scan the hills and
woods about him. He saw a deer, but that was all.
On and up he climbed until at last there were no
trees above him, only the peaks and the sky. Dusk
was beginning to settle. A flock of crows harried a
lone buzzard towards the mountains. He looked
about him for any sign of movement. There was
nothing, only the buzzard and he seemed to be
making for Spain, chased all the way by the
marauding crows. He disappeared over the peaks
and the crows seemed satisfied with that for
suddenly they broke off the chase and dispersed.

The sound of the shot came a moment later,
echoing around the mountains. Without that Jo
would never have seen the patrol. He crouched
down behind a rock. There were three of them,

three tiny dark figures moving slowly along the ridge against the skyline. A few of the crows settled on the ground now by Papa's hut and it occurred to him then that if Benjamin and Léah hadn't already been caught then they might be hiding up somewhere, and in that case there would be no better place than Papa's hut. The hut was several hundred metres away from him, built against a huge rock that had tumbled down the mountainside hundreds of years before. There were boulders strewn between him and the hut, boulders that he could use as cover; but even so he'd have to wait until the patrol had gone or until dark, whichever came first. For an hour or more the patrol moved slowly along the crest towards the Pic d'Anie and then the darkness thickened around him and he could see them no more.

The sliver of moon was for decoration only, it provided no light. It was safe enough to move now. Jo scuttled from boulder to boulder until he reached the hut. He whispered at the door as loud as he dared. 'Are you in there? Anyone in there?' But the reply came from behind him, from the donkey shed on the other side of the stream. It wasn't really a shed, just a cave in a rock with a half door across.

'Over here, Jo. We're over here.' It was Benjamin's voice.

He leapt the stream and picked his way over the rough ground towards the donkey shed.

'Inside!' said Benjamin opening the door and pulling Jo in. And then he saw Léah. She was backing away from him into the darkest corner of the shed. Benjamin limped after her leaning heavily on a stick.

'Don't mind her,' he said. 'She's frightened of her own shadow this one, but then she's got good cause.' It was some time before she could be persuaded to come out of her corner, and even then she wouldn't look at Jo but buried her head in Benjamin's coat. 'She's cold and she's tired, Jo,' he said, 'like me. We tried to cross last night. And we'd have made it too.'

'What happened?' said Jo.

'My ankle, my confounded ankle, that's what happened.' He stroked Léah's hair and hugged her close to him. 'We had the perfect night for it. Lots of clouds, plenty of wind; but soldiers, soldiers everywhere. I must have been over these mountains a dozen times now and I've never seen so many soldiers. That's why we were running. We don't normally run. It's always quieter if you walk. I don't know if it was a stone or a hole in the ground, it doesn't matter anyway. Somehow or other I turned my ankle over, you could hear it go – like a gunshot it was – and now it's blown up like a balloon. Anyway, we couldn't go on any further so all day we've been cooped up in here waiting for the soldiers to go. We were going to try to make it back on our own after dark, but I don't think we'd ever have done it, not on our own.'

'Is it broken?' Jo asked.

'Perhaps, but anyway it won't be much use to me

for a few months, that's for sure.' He bent over and kissed Léah on the top of her head. She looked up at him. 'It'll get better — God willing — and when it does we'll try again. I don't care how many soldiers they put on those mountains, we'll find a way past them. Now Jo,' he said, reaching out and putting a hand on his shoulder, 'I'm going to need someone strong to lean on.' He turned to Léah and spoke in another language. Léah looked from Benjamin to Jo and back again. Benjamin nodded and nudged her forward. She reached out slowly and Jo took her hand. 'All clear outside is it?' said Benjamin. Jo peered out. He could hear nothing and see nothing. He felt Léah's cold fingers gripping tighter.

'All clear,' he said, and with Benjamin's arm hooked around his neck they walked out into the night.

It was a slow and painful journey down the mountain. Benjamin may have been a small man but he was heavy enough and Jo's shoulder ached under his weight. He had to tread very carefully for he knew that if he stumbled they would all fall like a pack of cards. Léah clung to Jo's free hand and even on the narrowest tracks nothing could persuade her to let go and follow along behind. Any sudden jolt and Jo could hear the stifled groan, and feel the grip tighten around his shoulder. They stopped to rest by the river knowing that the worst part — the uphill part — still lay ahead. From now on Benjamin needed Léah too as a crutch, but even with one hand on her shoulder and an arm around Jo he had to put some weight on his useless foot. Every step was an agony to him, an agony Jo suffered with him.

Jo took them the quickest way up the hillside, across the open fields. There was no thought in his mind now of avoiding German patrols or of meeting anyone else for that matter; and clearly Benjamin felt the same for he began to sing, softly at first, through clenched teeth, and then within moments Léah's thin piping voice joined his. It was a slow, martial song, with a simple rhythmic tune that Jo soon picked up as well. That song with its regular, defiant beat kept them going all the way up to the house and by then they were singing out loud against the wind. A shadow came out from behind the barn and became Widow Horcada.

She took Benjamin's outstretched hand. 'We're all right, Grandmère,' he said, 'we're all right.' And Jo found himself suddenly and blissfully free of Benjamin's weight as Widow Horcada put her arms around him to support him.

'I'd better be getting back,' said Jo, rubbing his shoulder. 'They'll be wondering.'

'Bless you, Jo,' said Widow Horcada. It was the first time she'd ever called him 'Jo'.

'I told you, didn't I?' said Benjamin. 'I said this boy was a good one.' He bent down and whispered something to Léah.

'Dziękuję, Jo' she said, and her face broke at last into a shy smile.

'What does that mean?' Jo asked.

'It means "thank you" in Polish,' said Benjamin.

They were waiting up for him when he got home. Jo had made up his story on the way back. It wasn't difficult. It was a story he'd used often when he'd been late in, but then the story had often been true, or part of it anyway, and he'd never been this late. He'd seen the eagle again, he said, whilst he was out guarding the sheep and then Hubert had come along so he'd left him with the sheep. He'd followed the eagle all the way down the valley and up into the mountains to see if he could find its nesting site, then he'd lost his way in the dark on the way back. 'It's very dark out there,' he said.

Grandpère was frowning at him. 'Eagles don't nest in the Autumn, do they?' he said.

'Course not,' Jo went on, 'but I thought if I could find where it settled, then next Spring I'd know where to look. I've been looking for their nest for ages, you know I have.'

'Never mind about the eagle,' said Maman. 'What about the patrols? Didn't you hear what Monsieur Sarthol said. Didn't you? I've been worried sick, Jo.'

'I never saw anything,' said Jo.

'Your mother's told you. She's told you time and again, you're not to go off like that without telling her.' Grandpère was playing stern – he wasn't very good at it. 'You wouldn't have dared do it if your father was here, would you?' And Jo couldn't argue with that. He kept quiet, it was the best way. In the end they both ran out of admonishments as he knew they would, but more important they had not doubted his story and his secret was safe.

'Papa's written again,' said Maman pulling a card out of her pocket. They'd had cards like this before. It was a filled-in form, not a letter at all. Jo recognised Papa's handwriting. It said what all the others had said, that he was well, that he was still working in a timber yard and that was about all. 'Three years he's been gone now,' said Maman, 'nearly three years.'

'He'll be back Lise,' said Grandpère.

'Will he?' she said, shaking her head. 'Not if this war goes on like it is. They'll never let him come home, never.' Jo hated to see the tears in Maman's eyes and looked away. 'You know the worst thing,' she said, 'it's that I don't know where he is. If I knew where he was, if I could look at a map and say "he's there, that's where he is", that'd be something.'

'Off to bed, Jo,' said Grandpère, 'you've got school tomorrow. And no more chasing after your eagles, d'you hear me?' And he slapped Jo playfully on the bottom as he went out.

It was always the same whenever a card came from Papa. In between whiles they hardly ever talked about him. It wasn't that he was forgotten exactly. He just wasn't there, that's all. They'd all had to get along without him and they'd managed to do it partly because they didn't think about him; but whenever his cards came Maman would become morose and silent for days afterwards and that would upset everyone in the house, everyone except Grandpère – only the Germans seemed capable of upsetting Grandpère.

The next morning Hubert was waiting for him outside as he was most mornings. He liked to walk to school with Jo because he always had done. He was too old for school now but Monsieur Audap would let him sit at the back and make his miniatures. He even provided him with the bread. Hubert was never any trouble except for the occasional sound of spitting, and everyone ignored even that by now. Hubert's miniatures were made out of bread. He would cut open a loaf, pull out the soft bread and discard the crust. Then he would knead it into a thick paste, spitting on it all the time. He would roll it out until it was wafer thin and cut out the shapes he wanted. Somehow this unpromising material would be transformed into minute cups and bowls and chalices. When Hubert had finished modelling them, he would press them with the point of a hot iron until they were hard. It was a marvel that his great hands, that seemed often so clumsy, could produce such delicate work. Afterwards, when they had dried out, he would paint them with a fine brush, varnish them and then give them to his friends or to his father, whose house was full of them. Jo had twenty-one of them on the shelf in his bedroom, each one different from the other. They were a testament to a long and lasting friendship, and Jo treasured them.

Monsieur Audap liked to have Hubert in the

school, everyone did. There wasn't an ounce of
malice in him. The little children liked him because
he would let them climb on him at playtime. The
great game was to try and sit on Hubert to keep him
down, and he'd struggle and struggle and rise up
like a giant and discard them in all directions. Then
they'd climb on again and try to haul him down,
and in the end he'd let them, and they'd have their
triumph. The older children were half afraid of him
– Jo too if he was honest. Some, like Laurent, would
mock him occasionally, but only from behind his
back. And even then they respected him and not just
for his size but because Hubert was always game –
he would always join in whatever was going on. He
was like a chameleon; whatever they were – pirates,
soldiers, Red Indians – he would be too. When they
were happy, he was happy; and if someone was sad
then he'd sit beside them and share in their
wretchedness. And without exception everyone
admired his handiwork. Monsieur Audap said that
one day people would go to see it in an exhibition in
Paris, it was that good and no-one doubted it.

Hubert was sitting at the back of the class intent
on his latest minute bowl, his eyes close to his
fingers, when Armand Jollet burst into the
classroom. He took Monsieur Audap by the elbow
and led him towards the door. Both were talking in
excited whispers. Monsieur Audap saw him out and
then he called for Hubert, who was reluctant at first
to leave his bowl.

'Now, Hubert!' said Monsieur Audap clapping

his hands, and Hubert left his desk at once, wiping his hands on his trousers. 'The drum, Hubert,' he said and Hubert's eyes lit up; he loved his drum. For the children any interruption to lessons was always welcome, but when Hubert was being sent out around with the drum that meant something exciting had happened, something important even. By the time they were all gathered outside they could hear Hubert's drumming echoing around the village. Monsieur Audap lined them up in twos. They always went with the same partners. Jo went with Laurent, they had done since they were little, and they walked in a long crocodile down towards the Square. People were running out of their houses, pulling on their coats as they came. No-one knew what was going on, not until they reached the Square.

Soldiers were drawn up in front of the Mairie, two ranks of them in grey uniforms. They wore side caps not helmets. In front of them, on a bay horse, was an officer, both hands on his reins, a revolver in his belt. Hubert's drumming came ever closer as more people came crowding into the Square. Monsieur Sarthol, the tricolour of office around his waist, was standing beside the officer reading some papers. Jo found his view blocked so he climbed up on to the railings behind the war memorial just as Hubert, still drumming enthusiastically, came marching down into the Square. Grandpère, with Rouf beside him, was leaning against a wall studying the soldiers critically. The Mayor told

Hubert to stop, but Hubert was so intent upon his drumming that he did not hear his father's command. Armand Jollet tapped him on the shoulder and shook his head. Hubert stopped drumming. The officer waited until everyone was quiet before he began to speak. His accent was heavy but he spoke slowly and Jo could understand every word.

'My name is Lieutenant Weissmann,' he said. He spoke in a reedy voice, a voice that seemed to complement him perfectly. He was lean and long and lanky. 'I have been sent here to Lescun to guard this sector of the Frontier. My men and I will be billetted in the priest's house by the church. We will be living amongst you for some time and we wish to do so as peaceably as possible. I can assure you that we will not intrude into your lives unless you compel us to.' The horse tossed his head as the officer spoke, his bit jangling. He began to paw at the ground. The soldiers were not like the ones who'd come before. These were older men, some portly even, and with grey hair. Their boots were dusty and they looked somehow awkward in their uniforms. These were men dressed up as soldiers, not the real thing. The Lieutenant went on.

'There are certain rules, however, that must be obeyed. First, there will be a strict curfew. This means that after half past nine at night no-one is allowed out of their houses. Of course passes must be carried by everyone at all times. And lastly, all firearms, hunting rifles, shotguns and so on, must be handed in by six o'clock this evening – for safekeeping you understand. I repeat, we are here to guard the Frontier. Too many people have been escaping across into Spain. You all know what will happen if you are caught helping those wishing to escape. I have to tell you we want no unpleasantness but we have our job to do and we will do it. Thank you for your attention.' He pointed to the ground by the horse's feet. 'Six o'clock. You will leave your rifles here. My men will be here to receive them. That is all.' He turned to face the soldiers. There were barked commands and they marched across the Square and up the road towards the church, their rifles slung on their shoulders.

'I won't do it, Jo,' said Grandpère as they drove the sheep down from the fields later that afternoon. 'I won't do it I tell you. They march in here like they own the place. They kick Father Lasalle out of his house and tell us we mustn't go out after dark. What are we, children? Be good boys, hand in your guns. Who the hell do they think they are? Ah, they're polite enough these Germans. They say their pleases and afterwards they'll say their thankyous. All very polite I'm sure, but they can afford to be can't they?' It was a monologue that lasted all the way home.

Hubert was waiting for them kicking his heels on the wall. He jumped down to let the sheep in through the gate. At that moment three soldiers came round the corner, marching in step, their packs on their backs. They waited and watched as Hubert and Rouf drove the sheep into the yard. Jo saw that the tallest of them had stripes on his shoulders. He was head and shoulders above the others and wore his side cap at a jaunty angle. He had a drooping black moustache that was too small for his face. Jo caught his eye and the soldier smiled and waved at him cheerily; and then they were gone. Grandpère gripped his arm.

'Don't you go smiling at them,' he said. 'The last thing we want to do is make them feel at home.'

'I wasn't,' said Jo, and that was the truth. And yet he had wanted to return the smile. 'I was just looking,' he said.

The grip on Jo's arm tightened and Grandpère began to chuckle. 'They want rifles, don't they?' he said. 'Well, I'll give them a rifle. Wait here.' And he opened the gate and walked through the sheep into the barn. Moments later he came back out again and Jo understood at once what he was going to do. He was carrying the ancient muzzle-loading rifle they kept above the fireplace in the kitchen, the one his great grandfather had used in an old war a long time ago – or so the story went. He handed it to Hubert, who beamed and put it to his shoulder and aimed at a high flying crow. 'Bang,' he said. 'Bang, bang.'

'You can't give them that,' said Jo.

'And why not? It's what they asked for. They wanted rifles didn't they?' He turned to Hubert. 'It's not for you, Hubert; it's for them, for the

Boche.' And the smile left Hubert's face. 'Here, feel this Jo,' Grandpère went on, and he took Jo's hand and pressed it against his side. Jo could feel the barrel of his hunting rifle through the coat. 'Just in case they ever come searching – and they will, you can be sure of that – I'm going to hide this somewhere they'll never find it, somewhere they'll never even think of looking. Come on. You come too Hubert, I need you.' Hubert looked delighted again. He always loved to feel wanted, to feel useful.

They made their way up around the back of the village and came down behind the churchyard. Grandpère sat on the wall and looked about him, then he swung his legs over and let himself down the other side. The family tomb was on the far side of the graveyard overlooking the valley – the best view in the graveyard Grandpère always said. They crouched down behind the tomb and Grandpère opened his coat. He took the rifle out and leaned it carefully against a grey marble slab that served as the lid of the tomb.

'Here, give us a hand,' he said. The slab moved much more easily than Jo expected. 'That's far enough,' Grandpère said, looking around him. He plunged his hand into his coat pocket and came out with a single bullet. He held it up between his thumb and his forefinger. His voice was steely, as Jo had never heard it before. 'When the time comes, if the time comes, then at least I'll be taking one of them with me,' and he slipped the bullet in and rammed the bolt home. He wrapped it carefully in a cloth and let it down into the tomb, peering in after it. 'That'll do,' he said, and they heaved and shoved until the marble slab was back in place. 'Now,' said Grandpère wiping his hands together and grinning mischievously, 'now they can have their rifle. We'll give it to them personally.' And he picked up the ancient, rusted rifle, and they followed him through the back door of the church, down the dark aisle and out of the front door into the sunlight beyond.

There were two soldiers standing in the Square, half a dozen or so rifles lying on the ground at their feet. Grandpère walked right up to them. For several silent moments he looked them up and down, almost as if he was inspecting them, first one and then the other.

'Good evening,' he said at last. 'You wanted this, I believe,' and he laid the rifle down on top of the others.

The soldiers looked down at it and then at Grandpère; they seemed uncertain of what to do. 'It needs oiling from time to time,' said Grandpère. 'Make sure you look after it.' One of the soldiers was about to say something but Grandpère turned and walked away. When Jo looked back both the soldiers were gazing after them.

'I enjoyed that,' said Grandpère as they rounded the corner, and the smile on his face set Hubert laughing, and when Hubert laughed he laughed with his whole being and you had to laugh with him.

They were passing the baker's shop, Grandpère still chuckling, when Jo saw Widow Horcada. She was coming slowly towards them, her head down so you could only see the top of her shawl. She had a basket over each arm.

Grandpère held out his arms. 'Alice,' he shouted. 'You're looking younger than ever.'

She smiled as he came towards her. He kissed her warmly on both cheeks. 'Go on with you, you old goat,' she said, pushing him away, and then she looked at him quizzically. 'What're you looking so pleased about anyway?'

'That's our little secret, isn't it boys?' said Grandpère, taking Widow Horcada's arm. 'We're all allowed our little secrets, eh?'

She tried to shake him off. 'Henri! What will people think?'

'Let them think what they like,' said Grandpère. 'I'm too old to care and so are you.' Madame Soulet was at the door of her baker's shop, her mouth open. Grandpère bowed at her with a flourish. 'I shall carry your shopping, Madame. I shall escort you home.'

At that moment they heard the sound of laughter and a couple of soldiers came out of the Square towards them. They stopped at the corner to light each other's cigarettes.

'I heard they were here,' said Widow Horcada. 'How many of them are there?'

'There's twenty-two of the beggars,' said Grandpère, 'and a horse. They mean business. I tell

70

you one thing, no-one's ever going to get over those mountains again, not now.'

'That's your grandson isn't it?' said Widow Horcada. Jo dared not look her in the eye. 'Doesn't have much to say for himself does he?' Grandpère nudged him.

'Good morning, Madame,' said Jo.

'Strong boy is he?'

'Course he is,' said Grandpère and he squeezed Jo's shoulder approvingly. 'From good stock he is.'

The Widow Horcada nodded. 'You wouldn't like to lend him to me?' she said, wrinkling her nose and sniffing.

'Lend him?'

'Once a week say. He could bring me my shopping. It's climbing these hills, Henri – down's worse than up. My old knees aren't what they were.'

'I don't know,' said Grandpère. 'It's a bit difficult just at the moment, what with his father being away. Don't know if we can spare him.'

'I'll tell you what I'll do,' said Widow Horcada. 'I'll pay him, a kilo of honey every week. How's that? It won't take but an hour or two. Help me out it would.'

'Once a week you say?' said Grandpère. 'Well, I expect we could manage that. What do you think, Jo?' Jo nodded. 'When would you want him to start?'

'Now,' said Widow Horcada, and she held out the largest basket. 'Well, come along boy, I won't eat you. Come along.'

Grandpère laughed as they walked away. 'Mind you pay him now,' he called after them; and Jo followed the Widow in silence out of the village.

They were off the track and into the fields before she said a word. She put down her basket and bent over, her hands on her knees, breathing hard.

'Are you all right?' Jo asked.

She nodded and looked up. 'I'm sorry, Jo,' she said. 'But you're the only one that knows, you're the only one I could ask. It's not that I don't trust your grandfather but the fewer that know the less dangerous it is.' She straightened up slowly. 'We've got five of them now, Jo. Five children to look after, and there's more on the way. Benjamin's still laid up with his ankle; he can't even stand up, but even if he was fit they'd never make it over the mountains, not now, not with all these soldiers about. What can we do? We can't send the children back where they've come from, and we can't take them where they want to go.' She fanned her face with the corner of her shawl. 'I don't know what I'm going to do, Jo. I don't know how long I can keep them all fed. And that Armand Jollet at the shop, he's becoming suspicious, I know he is. You can't blame him – I've never bought so much in all my life; and what I do buy I can't carry, not on my own, Jo. I'm just not strong enough any more. I'm going to need all the help you can give me.'

Chapter Five

Hostility towards the German occupiers was silent, but as time passed they were proving more and more difficult to hate. They were tactful, unobtrusive even. No houses had been searched. No foreign flags of occupation fluttered over the village. Lieutenant Weissmann seemed as good as his word. The two communities existed side by side separately, ignoring each other respectfully. Some of the soldiers came to church on Sundays, Lieutenant Weissman amongst them. Father Lasalle loved to play the organ and it seemed that Lieutenant Weissmann shared his passion. Father Lasalle was only too pleased to let him practise on the church organ. Many of the soldiers came to the café in the evening but even there they sat apart, at first anyway. It soon became apparent though that two or three of them had fought at the Battle of Verdun in the First World War and it was not long before ancient enemies were exchanging reminiscences across the café, and with no rancour on either side. On the contrary their shared suffering seemed to banish mutual reserve and suspicion.

Jo wouldn't have believed it possible had he not witnessed it himself but even Grandpère was drawn into a moment of nostalgic self-indulgence. Jo was coming out of school one lunchtime when he caught sight of Grandpère outside the café. He was deep in conversation with a German soldier. He towered over Grandpère, a great tree of a man. He had stripes on his uniform, a Corporal, Grandpère had said. Besides Lieutenant Weissmann, the Corporal was the only soldier who spoke good French and he lost no opportunity to practise it on the children with whom he had already become a firm favourite, mostly because he seemed to have an endless supply of sweets. He had offered one to Jo only a few days before. Jo had taken it but then his conscience had got the better of him and he spat it out around the corner, something he immediately regretted as he watched Rouf enjoying it instead.

The Corporal smiled at Jo as he saw him coming and Grandpère looked somewhat shamefaced. On the way home he explained.

'It's hard to believe,' he said, 'but that Corporal and me, we were very likely shooting at each other at Verdun.' He shook his head. 'Just sixteen he was then. Invalided out same as me.' And then he caught Jo's eye and was silent.

This reunion of old soldiers broke the last of the ice and thereafter the village settled and adapted to the new normality of being occupied.

Hubert had seemed more resentful than most at first, and because he had no inhibitions was by far the most daring. He was always blowing raspberries at them in the street but the Germans simply laughed and blew raspberries back at him. It became a tit-for-tat game that Hubert enjoyed and they enjoyed. Before long they all knew his name. They would give him chocolate and they let him groom Lieutenant Weissmann's horse. Hubert was happy, and whoever made Hubert happy struck a common chord with the spirit of the village.

Jo had never much liked Armand Jollet before he shot the bear and he liked him even less now. With the arrival of the Germans his shop was doing well, very well. The soldiers had money to spend and nowhere else to spend it but the café and the shop. The Jollet family owned them both. No-one else in the village stooped to fawning except Armand Jollet. He would always accompany the soldiers to the door of his shop and open it for them. He would bow and scrape in a manner that made Jo cringe to watch him; and these days Jo was often in the shop to pick up Widow Horcada's provisions. Twice a week it was now, in all weathers, he climbed the hillside, his arms aching under the weight of the baskets. There were eight children up there now Widow Horcada told him. Jo had never set eyes on any of them except Léah and he hadn't seen her for some time. He longed to sneak into the barn and take a look but he knew he shouldn't. It was Benjamin who usually came to the door to take the baskets from him. He was still hobbling on his bad ankle. Jo was always invited in but he was never allowed to stay for long in the warmth of the kitchen. 'Your honey, Jo,' the Widow would say, pushing it across the table towards him. 'And here's the list for next time.' And then he'd find himself out in the yard again facing a closed door. He knew why he could not stay. Being inclined to repeat herself she had told him several times. 'You've got to remember, Jo,' she'd said, 'to everyone in the village you're just an unwilling delivery boy for the Black Widow. God knows who's watching your comings and your goings, but that's just what you must do, come and go. We don't want people asking questions do we? It's best that way.' Jo knew she was right but it hurt him just the same; and questions were beginning to be asked anyway, questions he could not answer.

One afternoon that winter, Monsieur Jollet caught him by the arm as he was leaving the shop: 'You know what she's doing with all this food?' Jo looked away. 'She's up to something isn't she?'

At that moment the door opened and the Corporal came in, his moustache white with snow. 'Jo, isn't it?' he said, stamping the snow off his boots. 'Whenever I see you, you are carrying those baskets. You have a big family?' Jo said nothing.

'It's for Madame Horcada, Corporal,' said

Armand Jollet. 'Jo does her fetching and carrying for her. She lives on her own but there's food enough there for a family of ten. I think she's storing it up for the winter, like a squirrel.' And he laughed a high-pitched, nervous laugh. 'And how can I help you, Corporal?'

'Cigarettes,' said the Corporal and then he turned to Jo. 'One minute, Jo, I'll give you a hand. It's slippery out there.' The Corporal paid for his cigarettes, Armand Jollet counting out his change rather too meticulously and finishing with a flurry of thankyous before showing them out.

The snow floated down in huge flakes. The Corporal insisted on carrying both the baskets. He had his head back and his tongue out to catch the snowflakes. He caught several before he got one in the eye and broke into laughter. 'It makes me feel as if I am at home,' he said. Jo walked along beside him searching his mind for some way of extricating himself from the situation.

'This Widow,' said the Corporal, 'where does she live?'

'Up in the hills outside the village,' Jo said and he reached for the baskets. 'I can manage, honestly I can.' But the Corporal would not let him take them.

'How far?'

'Three, maybe four kilometres.'

'That's not so far,' said the Corporal and they walked on. 'Bavaria, you know it?' Jo shook his head. 'In Germany, in the south of Germany. It's where I live, in a village like this, like Lescun. There are mountains all about just like these. I'm a forester, Jo, so for me you understand this is like home.'

Jo was desperately trying to think of a way to get rid of him. 'If she sees you,' said Jo, 'I won't get my honey.' It was weak but it was all he could think of.

'Honey?'

'She pays me. Widow Horcada, she pays me in honey, and if she sees you carrying the baskets for me she won't pay me.'

'I haven't had honey since I left home,' said the Corporal. 'Acacia honey and apple blossom honey, that's what we have at my home. My wife, she makes it. Of course the bees make it but she looks after the bees. And my children, they love it. They eat it so fast I am lucky if they leave me the spoon to lick. They're all girls, my children. Three of them. Can you imagine that, Jo? Four girls in one house and me? No honey and no peace.' His face was suddenly serious. 'I never thought I'd miss them so much. One of them, she has gone to Berlin to work the telephones. She's the clever one.' He stopped and put down the baskets. 'These baskets, they are heavy. There is enough in here to feed the five thousand.'

Jo saw his opportunity and picked them up at once. 'Thanks,' he said. 'I can take them now.'

'Very well,' said the Corporal, 'but one day, one day I must taste your honey, yes?' He looked up through the falling snow at the mountains around them. 'I am like a bear,' said the Corporal laughing.

'I like honey, and I like mountains. I like snow. We have bears in my mountains too you know; and eagles, we have eagles.'

'So have we,' said Jo.

'I know,' said the Corporal. 'I have seen them, and vultures too. Have you ever seen eagles through binoculars, Jo?'

'No.'

'In the Spring, Jo, we go up the mountains together, you and me; and we look at eagles with my binoculars, yes? With binoculars you can see an eagle close as your nose, just like you can reach out and touch it. It's a promise, yes?' And the Corporal turned and walked away.

Once inside the warmth of the farmhouse Jo did not want to leave, and for a change they did not seem to want him to either. They sat him down over a bowl of hot soup which he blew on to steam his face warm. He had almost finished wiping his bread around the bowl when he realised that no-one was saying anything. With his mouth still full of bread he looked from one to the other and waited. It was clear they had something to tell him.

'Jo,' said Benjamin, 'I know you have done a lot for us already,' and as he spoke he walked slowly over to the stove, leaning for support on the backs of the chairs as he went. He turned round and faced him, his face serious, 'and we don't like to ask you.'

'Ask me what?'

'We need money, Jo,' said Widow Horcada. 'We just haven't got the money to go on buying food.

There's ten of them in the barn now. They've eaten me out of house and home. The cow's gone dry so there's no milk any more. I haven't even got any honey left to pay you. I've got enough money to last another week and that'll be the end of it.' She sank back in her chair. 'There's only one thing we can do, Jo. I've got to sell my pigs. The children won't eat them and Benjamin won't eat them – it's against their religion – and I can't afford to go on feeding them. With the money they make we can go on for a few more months maybe. So they'll have to go. But I'm not selling them to anyone, Jo. Those pigs, they're like family to me. There's only one other person knows enough about pigs in this valley and that's Henri, your Grandfather. Always used to keep pigs when he was a young man and he was good at it too. The trouble is he's not going to buy them without seeing them is he? And that's what I want you to do, Jo. I want you to bring him up here.' Jo looked across at Benjamin. 'Don't you worry nothing about him,' Widow Horcada went on, 'he'll be well out of sight, same as the children. Henri won't know anything, and what he won't know can't hurt him, can it? So, the next time you come up here with the shopping – that'll be next Wednesday afternoon won't it? – I want you to bring your Grandfather with you.'

'What am I going to tell him?' asked Jo.

'Tell him I'm too old, tell him I can't get about like I used to – that'll be true enough. Tell him what you like, Jo, but get him here.'

'Can you do it, Jo?' Benjamin said.

'I'll try,' said Jo.

And he tried that evening whilst Maman was upstairs putting Christine to bed.

'What? All of them?' said Grandpère, and he was frowning as he lit his cigarette and coughed the match out.

'That's what she told me,' said Jo. 'She told me she's too old to go on.'

Grandpère shook his head. 'Doesn't make sense. Doesn't make sense any of it. She's always had pigs up there, and her father before her. She loves those pigs like her own children. She'd never sell them, not unless she had to, I know she wouldn't. I tell you, Jo, if she gives up her pigs that'll be the end of her. She'll have nothing left to live for.'

'Perhaps she needs the money,' said Jo.

'Well I'd like to know what for,' Grandpère said, 'after all, she's only got herself to look after hasn't she? She's been careful all her life. I just can't understand it. Still,' he said, smiling through the cigarette smoke, 'that's the first invitation I've had from her in nigh on fifty years so I'll go.' He leaned forward and spoke low. 'But don't you go telling your mother, Jo. She doesn't like her, and what's worse she doesn't like me to like her. There's stories about me and the old Widow – not true of course – but if I know your mother she'll start thinking her thoughts, so not a word, eh?' Jo was quite used by now to keeping secrets. One more would not be that difficult.

Rouf followed them that Wednesday afternoon but Jo did not notice him until it was too late. He tried to send him back but he wouldn't go. You could never make Rouf do anything he didn't want to do. They were walking across Widow Horcada's back yard when he saw Rouf sniffing along the barn wall towards the door. When he reached it he stopped, his nose thrust under the door and snuffling noisily. Then he began to scratch at it and whine.

'What's up with that dog?' said Grandpère and then the door of the house opened and Widow Horcada was there.

'I'll take those,' she said looking at Jo hard, and she almost snatched the baskets out of his hands. 'You can take that dog home, Jo.' She spoke sharply. 'You know I don't like dogs around my place.' She looked at Grandpère. 'Well, don't just stand there, Henri, come along in and shut the door behind you.'

It was all Jo could do to drag Rouf away from the barn door. He had to drive him down the hillside from behind like a sheep. Jo would have given anything to stay behind and listen to what was going on. He wondered where Benjamin would be hiding – in the barn perhaps, with the children, he thought, to keep them calm. If so, then Rouf's snuffling must have shaken them all rigid. But wherever they all were they must have kept well hidden, and whatever money arrangements they came to inside the house must have been satisfactory for Grandpère was quite evidently delighted when he came back. He told Maman that evening that pigs would be in great demand now. The Boche eat a lot of pork. He could fatten them on the sheeps' whey for practically nothing. He would hardly have to buy any feed for them, he said. 'But they smell,' Maman protested. 'Pig smell, you can never wash it off.' But Grandpère managed to persuade her it was a smell they could learn to live with. Christine was delighted with the idea – she'd never ridden a pig.

The next day as Jo came tramping home from school through the village he saw Hubert and Grandpère coming down the road driving the pigs in front of them, or trying to. It was all going fine until they reached the Square and the pigs set off at a trot. They went running off in all directions, squealing and grunting as they explored every front door and every drainpipe. It took half the village and a few of the soldiers as well to round them all up and drive them back to Jo's house where they managed to pen them all in, all except one – a large determined sow with pink and swinging teats – that Jo had to chase all the way to the church and back before she at last gave up and reluctantly joined her friends.

Grandpère's new pigs had become the talk of the village. After church on Sunday there were dark whisperings that Henri Lalande had bought the Widow's pigs for reasons that were not entirely agricultural or commercial. There was much tutting and shaking of heads and some smirking mirth too. Jo overheard Madame Soulet in the street saying that Henri Lalande must be out of his mind. 'At his age!' she said. 'At his age!'

At school Laurent snorted at Jo now whenever he met him, and 'oink oink' became the new greeting amongst the children until the joke wore thin. Maman declared that the sheep were giving less milk now that the pigs were about the place, but Grandpère just smiled and said that they'd soon settle down; and sure enough they did.

With the end of the snows the sheep were being moved each day to and from the pastures around the village and the sound of their bells in the fields heralded the first edelweiss and the first larks. You didn't have to go out into the countryside though to know it was Spring. When Father Lasalle left the church door open so that the sound of his organ playing could be heard all over the village, everyone knew for sure that Winter was behind them.

Monsieur Audap took advantage of the warming sun to lead the class out on the Spring expedition. He did this once for every season of the year, and the children looked forward to it more even than a holiday. It was like a treasure hunt. They scoured the slopes looking for plants and insects, footprints and droppings. Everything they found was recorded and sketched. There wasn't a plant Monsieur Audap could not name, nor a footprint nor a dropping he could not identify.

The great find of the day was a bear print in the

muddy beach down by the river. It was Laurent who found it first – Laurent found most things first. Everyone thought it was another of his practical jokes. 'A bear!' he cried. 'It's got to be.' And Monsieur Audap confirmed it. 'A front paw,' he said, 'and a small one at that; but it's a bear right enough, a young one I'd say. Look at the claw marks.'

'What's the matter, Jo?' said Laurent clapping him on the back. 'You look as if you've seen a ghost.' They hunted up and down the river bank for more prints but they found none. 'A one-footed bear,' said Laurent hopping beside Jo on the way back that afternoon, but Jo found it difficult to enjoy the joke. 'Cheer up Jo,' he said. Jo smiled as best he could but it was not very convincing and he knew it.

They sang songs all the way back to the village, Monsieur Audap waving his hand above his head conducting them. As they came round the last bend in the road they saw a German patrol coming towards them. 'Sing up, sing up,' said Monsieur Audap, and they swung past the patrol in full voice. Jo enjoyed the moment, they all did. It was a little victory but even a little victory was better than none at all.

They were still in high spirits when they came into the village. Perhaps that was why Laurent put his tongue out at Madame Soulet as she was arranging baguettes in the window of her shop. She came rushing out after Monsieur Audap complaining bitterly and pointing at Laurent. After they got back to school Laurent was called into Monsieur Audap's room and Jo noticed that when he came out he was only just smiling. Monsieur Audap had clearly said his piece – and he had a way of reaching his mark.

It was that interview that goaded Laurent into an act of revenge and for that he needed an accomplice.

'I need someone with a deep voice, Jo,' he said, 'and that means you.' It was never easy to say no to Laurent. Always good friends, with both their fathers prisoners-of-war in Germany, they had become even closer allies. Jo was left with no choice in the matter. 'We'll meet at my place,' said Laurent, 'just before curfew.'

'What for?' Jo asked.

'For a bit of fun,' Laurent said. 'I'll teach the old bat. I'll teach her.'

Jo knew well enough which 'old bat' he was talking about but until he got to Laurent's house that night he had no idea what she was going to be taught.

'I can see her from my window. I've watched her,' said Laurent. 'She always comes out of Madame Robbé's house between twenty past and half past nine. She walks across the Square and then back to her place, regular as clockwork. You know what you've got to do?' Jo didn't want to do it, not because he didn't dare – there was nothing very daring about it – he just didn't think they could pull it off; but Laurent ignored all his doubts and protests.

Laurent tested the torch and they crept out together into the dark streets. Once in place they crouched down behind a wall and waited. Jo had been rehearsed in his part but as the door of the Robbé's house opened and he heard Madame Soulet's shrill voice he found that his brain was suddenly frozen, that he could no longer remember his words. The door closed plunging the Square into darkness again. The moment had come. Laurent waited until the footsteps were just the other side of the wall and then he stood up, shining his torch directly into Madame Soulet's eyes. Laurent had to kick Jo into action. Jo cleared his throat.

'*Halt,*' he said in his deepest voice. '*Ihre Papiere bitte.*' And then in his best guttural German accent, 'Your papers please.' Jo looked up from his crouching position under the wall. Madame Soulet was holding up her hand trying to keep the light out of her eyes and she was stammering with terror. She held out her papers, her hand trembling. Laurent took them, glanced at them perfunctorily and handed them back quickly. '*Gut, sehr gut,*' said Jo as rehearsed. '*Gute Nacht.*' And she hurried away whimpering into the dark, Laurent's torch beam following her all the way to her door. When she had gone in Laurent bent over the wall and put his hands over his mouth to stop himself laughing out loud. Jo took the torch out of his hand and switched it off.

'Did you see her face?' said Laurent. 'Did you see it? You were brilliant, Jo, brilliant.' And then from the darkness behind them came a soft voice.

'*Ausgezeichnet.*' Jo's heart leapt into his mouth. 'A brilliant performance as you said.' They turned and the torch beam hit their faces full on. '*Ihre Papiere bitte,*' said the voice. It was Lieutenant Weissmann.

'I haven't got them on me,' said Laurent.

'*Und du?*' The torch came full beam on Jo's face. Jo shook his head. He could just make out a shadow behind the torch and the outline of a head against the sky. 'Turn around,' said Lieutenant Weissmann. They obeyed. '*Hände Hoch.* Hands up.' He kicked Laurent first and Jo waited for his turn. When it came it was more than a playful kick in the pants. It hurt just enough to carry a meaning. 'Do not do it again,' said Lieutenant Weissmann. 'You understand me? You have one and a half minutes before curfew. *Schnell!*' They climbed the wall and ran home going their different directions. Jo did not stop until he'd shut the door behind him and even then his heart could not stop pounding in his ears.

Whenever Jo went up to Widow Horcada's farm with the shopping now Benjamin would put on his shawl and come out into the yard to see him off. He would walk up and down to show him how much he was improving and each time he walked more easily. First the stick went and then within weeks the limp was almost gone. He even tried running on it but only for a few steps. 'It won't be long now, Jo,' he said. 'We'll soon have the children away.' Every time Jo asked how many children there were the figure increased.

'We've sent word,' said Widow Horcada. 'Time and again we've told them not to send any more down the line but the children keep coming. There's twelve of them now.'

And suddenly Benjamin was never there any more. For weeks, months, Jo never saw him at the house. Whenever he asked after him Widow Horcada would say he was in the barn with the children, or she would simply pretend not to hear; and when she did that Jo never quite dared to probe any further. He never saw any sign either of the children. Every time he passed the barn he longed to take a look inside; it was so difficult to imagine there were twelve children living in there.

They hardly saw anything of Grandpère these days. He'd leave first thing in the morning. 'Off up to work on the hut,' he'd say. Apparently there was a lot of storm damage, a great hole in the roof and all the shutters had to be replaced. It was the same every morning. 'You'll have to manage the sheep without me,' he'd say. 'I'll be back before dark.'

Hubert was always there to help Jo with the milking. He caught sheep better than anyone Jo knew. He seemed to understand them, to know which way they were thinking of going. His timing was perfect, stretching out his long arm and catching a back leg with consummate ease.

One morning, with Grandpère gone up to the hut again, the two of them had finished milking the flock and were taking the milk to Jo's mother in the kitchen when they heard a knock on the door. Jo answered it. A German soldier was standing there and there was another behind him.

'Orders of Lieutenant Weissmann,' he said, looking over Jo's shoulder into the house. 'We are searching all the houses.'

'What for?' said Maman coming to the door. Jo wasn't sure if the soldier understood or not for he did not reply.

'Entschuldigung,' said the soldier and he walked past them into the kitchen and up the stairs, his boots heavy on the boards above them. There were sounds of furniture being dragged across the floor. Hubert looked alarmed. Maman put a hand on his arm and held it. 'It's all right, Hubert,' she said. 'It's all right. We've got nothing to hide.' The soldier came down the stairs again and went through the kitchen into the barn. Jo followed him. The sheep took fright and packed against the far wall.

'I've got to take the sheep out,' said Jo pushing past the soldier. The soldier shook his head. He clearly did not understand. Jo spoke louder, pointing. 'The sheep, I must put them out. They must eat.' The soldier shrugged his shoulders. Jo had only one thought. Somehow he had to get up to the Widow Horcada's house and warn them. *All* the houses, the soldier had said, they were searching *all* the houses.

The sheep moved infuriatingly slowly out of the village that morning and Rouf was proving even more lethargic than usual. Several times they came to a complete halt bunching tight together in the streets. Only Hubert's loudest whooping managed to shift them and it was some time before the sheep were up in their pastures and grazing. As soon as they were settled Jo left them with Hubert and Rouf and made for Widow Horcada's farm, running. Half-way up the hillside he paused for breath and looked back down towards the village. A soldier on horseback was riding along the road towards where Hubert was sitting on the rock. Lieutenant Weissmann, it had to be — he was the only one who ever rode the horse. There were two soldiers walking along behind him. Jo ducked into the trees, he'd have to keep under cover all the way to the farm. It would take longer but he had no choice. He did not stop again until the back of the house was below him and he was sure he could not be seen from the road below. He raced down across the yard and threw open the door. Widow Horcada was sitting in her chair, her mouth gaping. Her eyes flickered. There was someone behind the door. Jo turned to look. Grandpère was standing there, his arms raised above his head and there was an iron in his hands.

Chapter Six

Grandpère lowered the iron. 'What the devil are you doing here, Jo?'

It was a moment or two before Jo could catch his breath. 'They're coming,' he said. 'The soldiers, they're coming this way. They're searching all the houses.'

'You sure?' said Grandpère going to the window.

'I'm sure,' Jo said.

'Well,' said Widow Horcada. 'You told us it would happen, Henri, and it has. It's what we planned for isn't it?'

'You'll be all right will you?' Grandpère said pulling on his coat.

'Of course we will,' she said. 'Now get going and be quick about it.' Grandpère had the back door open by now. 'And Henri, don't come back till we come for you. If we don't come you'll know the worst and you'll know what to do.' Grandpère made to come back into the room. 'No goodbyes,' said Widow Horcada and she waved him away. 'Just go.' And the door closed behind him. 'Come here, Jo,' she said and she took his hand. 'How far away are they?'

'They were down on the road,' said Jo. 'Five minutes, maybe ten, but they could be going further down the valley to Mougin's place or maybe . . .'

'They'll be here. Sooner or later they'll be here,' said the Widow. 'We'll plan on sooner. Now, everyone knows you go shopping for me?' Jo nodded. 'That's what you've come for then, money for the shopping. Here.' She stood up and took a few coins from the mantlepiece. 'Take it,' she said. 'And you'll be eating when they come. Boys are always eating aren't they? So, fetch a plate and a knife and cut yourself some bread. We'll keep it natural. I'll be knitting, you'll be eating.'

'But what about the children?' asked Jo.

'Just you let me do the worrying,' she said. 'All you've got to do is eat.' And Widow Horcada gathered her stitches and busied herself over her knitting. 'I've done ten of these jumpers now,' she said, 'all sizes.' But Jo wasn't thinking of the children any more.

'Why was Grandpère here?' he said. Widow Horcada did not answer. 'Does he know all about Benjamin, about Anya, about the children?' The Widow looked up from her knitting.

'I didn't want to tell him,' she said. 'He guessed most of it and I had to tell him the rest. He's no fool, your grandfather, not an easy man to lie to – never was. You remember that day you brought him up here? Well, he kept on at me about why I needed the money. He had to know the truth he said or else he wouldn't help me, so I had to tell him.'

'About me too?' said Jo.

'Everything,' she said. 'Now look what you've made me do, I've dropped my stitches again.' She was still trying to gather them when they heard the snorting of a horse outside and the sound of hooves on the cobbles. 'Eat, Jo, eat.' whispered Widow Horcada and Jo stuffed a crust of bread in his mouth and chewed on it. Somehow it helped to control the fear rising in the pit of his stomach. There were voices outside now, a barked command and then the expected knock on the door. Widow Horcada waited for a few moments, put her knitting in her lap and composed herself.

'Come in,' she said, and the door opened.

Lieutenant Weissmann clicked his heels. He was very tall in the room, his head almost touching the beams. 'Pardon Madame,' he said looking around the room, 'but we are carrying out searches.'

'Are you indeed?' said Widow Horcada coldly. 'And what is it that you are searching for, may I ask?'

The Lieutenant smiled. 'We shan't know that, Madame,' he said, 'until we find it, shall we?' He ushered a soldier past him and pointed to the staircase, then he turned his gaze on Jo. 'And what are you doing here?' he asked. Jo found he couldn't speak so he didn't try.

'He does my shopping for me, don't you, Jo?'

'Ah yes,' said Lieutenant Weissmann studying him hard; and he turned again to the Widow. 'You live here alone?'

'Yes,' said Widow Horcada. 'My husband was killed in the last war. I am quite alone.'

'I am sorry, Madame,' said the Lieutenant.

'Sorry? And what is it that you are sorry for Lieutenant? That I am a widow? That I am alone? Or that you are searching my house and treating me like a common criminal? Which?'

'*Entschuldigung* Madame,' said the Lieutenant stiffly, and he called upstairs: '*Etwas?*'

'*Nein Herr Oberleutnant,*' and the soldier's boots were heavy on the staircase as he came back down into the kitchen.

'And what do you keep in your barn, Madame?' said the Lieutenant.

'Animals,' she said, sniffing and wrinkling her nose. 'Farmers usually keep animals in barns, it's what they're for. Before I sold them I used to keep my pigs in there through the Winter.'

'And now?'

'Nothing, some hay for my cow, that's all.'

'Then you won't mind if we take a look?' said Lieutenant Weissmann.

'Lieutenant,' she said. 'Let us not play games with each other. You will search my barn whether I want you to or not.'

'Indeed, Madame, but I only meant . . .'

Widow Horcada interrupted him. 'I know what you meant. Do it, Lieutenant. Just do what you have to do and leave us in peace.'

'*Auf Wiedersehen* Madame,' he said and they left, shutting the door behind them.

Jo ran to the window. One of the soldiers was pushing at the barn door. He kicked it and it flew open.

'They're going in,' said Jo. 'They'll find them.'

'No they won't, Jo,' said the Widow. 'They won't find anything because there's nothing in there but hay, bracken and a lot of old pigs' muck.'

'Then where are they?' said Jo.

'Come away from that window,' said Widow Horcada smiling. 'And you can put my money back before you forget.' She took his hand as he passed her. 'You're a brave boy, Jo. It's a funny thing you know, but when you're old and used up like I am and there's only the grave to look forward to, nothing seems to frighten you very much.' They heard the barn door shut and the horse moving off. 'We'll wait for an hour or so just to be sure,' she said, 'then we'll go and find them.'

'Where are they?' asked Jo again.

'You'll find out soon enough,' she said.

It was a long silent climb up through the trees. Widow Horcada walked ahead of him, pausing every so often for breath. There must be no talking, she had said, not one word. All the time Jo was trying to guess where the children might be. They

96

were heading up towards the plateau. There were several shepherd's huts up there and some of them would certainly be large enough to house the children. He could not think of anywhere else they might be. Where the mountain met the tree line the trees grew more sparsely. There was more daylight above them now. Jo looked up. A few spindly trees clung for life to the rock face above him. Widow Horcada stopped and leaned on her stick. She looked about her, listening, her finger to her lips; and then she was bending and pulling aside the undergrowth. Behind the bracken and the brambles was a curtain of sacks. She lifted it and beckoned Jo through after her. Jo ducked down and found himself in darkness. She had him by the wrist and was leading him along what seemed to be a passage and Jo was groping ahead of him like a blind man. A single light glowed dimly far ahead of him. Then there were several lights, lights that were suddenly bright and flickering as another curtain of sacks parted in front of them. Grandpère was there, holding out his hand to help him in and Benjamin was beside him. A young girl clung to Benjamin's arm and Jo saw at once that it was Léah. He wasn't sure she even recognised him at first, but then her eyes lit up. 'Jo,' she said, and she took his hand at once as if he belonged to her and led him deeper into the cave.

The cave was narrow, low and long, and dimly lit with guttering lamps hung here and there along the walls. At first glance it was not always easy to distinguish the children from their own shadows. The place smelt of oil and cheese and meadow hay. Everywhere the floor was covered with bracken, except for a great bed of hay in the darkest corner where a huddle of children were curled together in sleep.

Along a winding track in the bracken came a wooden train propelled towards him by two boys on their knees, one chuffachuffing and the other oo-ooing. Then the wagons became unhitched and there was an instantaneous quarrel. Benjamin crouched down beside them to make the peace which was achieved as soon as the train was linked together again. Jo recognised it then as his own train, the battered train of his childhood – he hadn't set eyes on it for years. He looked back at Grandpère who smiled and shrugged his shoulders. 'Didn't think you'd mind,' he said. Three girls sat side by side over the same book, the girl in the middle reading aloud to the other two, one of whom turned the page to see for herself what would happen next. The reader snatched her hand back and held on to it for a moment before taking off her glasses and breathing on to them. It was then that she looked up and saw Jo. She froze. Quite suddenly all the children had noticed him. 'Jo,' Léah announced. She was introducing him. 'Jo.' The sleeping ones on the hay were nudged into consciousness. Jo felt the stare of each of them. It was more curiosity than hostility he thought, but there was suspicion enough in those looks to make him feel uncomfortable.

'Well Jo,' said Benjamin. 'What do you think of it? Three months I've been up here now. The children and me, we've made ouselves quite snug. We've got running water at the back of the cave. Your grandfather's idea it was. We've got a lot to thank him for.'

'I used to come up here a lot at one time,' Grandpère said. 'My father, your great-grandfather, Jo – God rest him – he used to do a bit of smuggling over the border – brandy mostly, everyone was at it in those days – and he kept his stuff in here. To tell you the truth I'd almost forgotten about the place until they showed me that barn full of children. If those soldiers had come looking during the Winter . . . well, it doesn't bear thinking about does it?'

'Then don't think about it, Henri,' said Widow Horcada lowering herself gingerly on to a wooden bench. 'No sense in thinking about what could have happened especially when it didn't.'

'Maybe, maybe not,' said Grandpère somewhat tersely. 'I'm telling you, Alice, today was a warning. I've told you before we've got to get these children out of here, and soon. I can take them. I know these mountains like the back of my hand.'

'And I've told you before, said Widow Horcada, 'you've got no patience, never have had. We've got to wait till the time is right. D'you think we want to keep the children here a minute longer than we have to? Do you? Benjamin's ankle may be better and the snow may be gone; but you tell me Henri Lalande, you tell me how we're going to take twelve children past those German patrols. You've seen them, they're everywhere, and anyway there's two or three children still too weak to make the journey.' Grandpère was about to argue. 'No, Henri, they're safer here. You said yourself no-one knows this place except you. We bide our time like we all agreed.'

'I was up in the mountains again only yesterday,' said Benjamin, 'looking for a way through. Two, maybe three times a week I'm up there studying the routes the patrols take, how often they come, when they come. I don't care how well you know them, Henri, you'd never make it. On your own maybe, if you're lucky, but not with all these children. We've got to wait. That's all we can do – wait and pray.'

Someone was tugging Jo's coat. He looked down. A small boy gripped his arm and dragged him away.

'That's Michael,' Benjamin called after him. 'He wants you to play chess. You won't stand a chance.'

From his size Jo thought Michael must be about half his age. Michael fell on his knees in the bracken and set out the pieces on a flat rock that served as a chessboard. The squares were marked out with white chalk. He held out his clenched fists and Jo knelt down and tapped his right hand. Black. Jo was happy. He always won with black. Jo was good at chess, so good Laurent wouldn't play him any more, nor would Grandpère. Only Monsieur Audap beat him regularly. Suddenly he was aware of shadows crowding in around him; all the other children were coming to watch. Michael never looked up at him once during the game. In between moves he sat with his arms folded, his eyes on the board, and when it was his turn he moved his piece without hesitation and without any apparent thought. After half a dozen moves Jo just wished it to be over. Every piece he lost provoked a sigh of pleasure from the audience and when a few minutes later Jo found himself checkmate, Michael looked up for the first time and smiled. Jo saw that when he smiled his ears moved and he could not help but smile back.

'You play better than your grandfather,' said Michael. 'I beat him in ten moves.'

It was little enough consolation for Jo as he went back down through the trees with Grandpère later that day. Grandpère was grumbling. 'She always argues, that woman. Trouble is she's always right too, and that only makes it worse. It's true enough what she says. There's patrols out everywhere, along the river, in the woods. Once up the top you could maybe slip past on a dark night; but between here and there you'd never do it, not with the children. There's got to be a way through, there's got to be.'

'Grandpère,' said Jo. 'Why didn't you tell me?'

'Tell you what?'

'You've been going up there all the time haven't you? Why didn't you tell me?'

Grandpère stopped and turned to him. 'Because

she told me not to, Jo. And she's right. It's safer not to know. Come to that, I could ask the same of you. You never told me, did you?'

'Same reason,' said Jo.

'There you are then,' said Grandpère and he smiled. 'I'm proud of what you've done, Jo, and Maman would be too; but not a word at home, Jo, not even a look. We don't talk about it at all. Not behind closed doors, not with a hundred bleating sheep around us. I don't want her knowing, Jo. You know how she worries.'

They walked on for a bit. 'That little boy, that Michael,' said Jo. 'He said he beat you in ten moves.'

'So he did,' said Grandpère, 'but he's hardly a little boy. Benjamin says he's nearly fifteen – same sort of age as you. Nothing much of him is there? That's what hunger does for you.'

The Germans found nothing in the village that day except for a couple of unusable rifles. For some weeks afterwards there was a frosty enmity between the villagers and the soldiers. Hubert blew his raspberries again and Laurent put his tongue out at them – when they weren't looking of course. Even Armand Jollet stopped opening doors for them. But time healed the wound and everyone was soon back on speaking terms again with the soldiers. There was a greater caution now and a new understanding, that harmless though they might seem, the soldiers were still the enemy and when called upon, they would behave like it.

Jo avoided all of them now, even the Corporal. Every time he saw them he could not put it out of his mind that these men were hunters. They were hunting down Benjamin and Léah, Michael and the others. Just to look at the soldiers made him feel uncomfortable; so he distanced himself from them, he accepted no sweets and exchanged no civilities.

At home, too, Jo felt uncomfortable. He had lived for a long time now with his secret and up till now had felt no sense of guilt at keeping it from Maman. But now that his secret had become a kind of conspiracy with Grandpère he found himself acting out a charade. It was hateful for him to have to lie to her, to watch her being constantly and successfully deceived. He found it more and more difficult to look her in the eye, to talk to her even, so he spent all the hours he could out with Rouf and Hubert looking after the sheep.

He was sitting on his rock with Hubert one morning when he saw the Corporal coming along the road. He had no rifle, only binoculars round his neck. He stopped and smoothed Rouf who did not discriminate at all – he liked anyone who adored him, Germans included.

'It's Friday,' the Corporal announced. 'On Fridays I have some hours off duty and I do not forget my promise.'

'Promise?' said Jo.

'The eagle, the binoculars. You don't remember?' Hubert was inspecting the binoculars closely. 'You want to look, Hubert?' said the Corporal. 'I show

103

you.' And he took off the binoculars and hung them around Hubert's neck. Hubert held them to his eyes and looked out across the valley. The Corporal tapped him on the shoulder and pointed upward. A lark hovered there noisily. A moment or two later Hubert found it in the binoculars and the Corporal focused it for him. Hubert roared with excitement. The Corporal laughed and patted him on the back.

'Well, Jo,' he said, 'do you want to come with me?'

'Take Hubert,' said Jo and he looked away.

'As you wish,' said the Corporal quietly, and he turned to Hubert. 'You come with me, Hubert?' and pointed towards the mountains. 'We look for eagles, yes?' He held his arms out wide. 'Eagles, high up.' He made binoculars out of his hands, put them to his eyes and scanned the mountains. 'Eagles,' he said flapping his arms. 'You come?' Hubert looked at Jo and then at the sheep.

'Go on,' said Jo. 'I'll mind them.' Rouf got up to go with them but Jo held him back; he needed the company.

He sat with his thoughts all that morning. He'd been up to the cave several times now with Grandpère and Widow Horcada, carrying oil and food, and each time he'd wondered at Benjamin's seemingly unshakeable optimism. The more he thought about it the more he could see no good reason for it. The days passed, the months passed and still Anya did not come. If she was alive after all this time – and like Widow Horcada Jo found that increasingly difficult to believe – then where was she and why hadn't she come? He never shared his misgivings with Benjamin, for in Benjamin's few unguarded moments Jo sensed a fragility in his faith that might not stand the test of reason. And besides, it was easier and more comforting to go along with Benjamin's repeated assurances. 'She'll be hiding up somewhere,' he'd said. 'Maybe in a barn, maybe in a cave just like ours. She'll come. God willing, she'll come. God looks after his own, Jo. He always does.' Jo hoped hard that he did.

News of the war was better. The Germans were being driven back out of Russia and out of Africa, but liberation was still a distant dream and a dream no-one dared talk of for fear that it still might not happen. Yet Jo could see no other hope for the children or for Benjamin. The patrols were just as frequent and watchful as ever; there always seemed to be some children sick and Benjamin would not hear of leaving any of them behind. 'We all go or we none of us go,' he said. 'Wait and pray. Our time will come.'

Jo would have liked to have made friends with the children in the cave. They all knew who he was by now but they still treated him like a stranger and hid themselves behind their dark eyes – all except Michael who never let him leave without beating him at chess. Michael had recently become one of the sick children. He had developed an abscess on his leg and a fever with it but it didn't stop him wiping Jo off the board every time in under twenty moves. The games were always held in complete silence, a rapt audience all around. Jo still chose black, believing and hoping that one day it would bring him luck, but it never did him any good. Widow Horcada would never let him stay very long after the game so there was not much time for talking, and when they did Michael was full of questions about Jo, about his family, about the animals on the farm, about his school. He would say little about himself, only that he could speak four languages, Polish, French, German and a little English. 'I want to speak ten,' he said. But he never once spoke of his family. Jo asked Widow Horcada where they all were and she would not tell him. 'There's some things better not to think about,' she said and nothing more was said about it; and Grandpère was no more forthcoming. Either they didn't know or they didn't want to talk about it, Jo was not sure which. But the more he thought about it the more he was convinced that they did know and that they were just not telling him. He wondered why. The sun was hot on his head and Jo felt like lying down, but he'd done that once before and he would never do it again. He talked to Rouf instead.

Some hours later, as he was moving the sheep further down the valley to fresh pastures, he saw the Corporal and Hubert walking across the field towards him. Hubert broke into a leaping run, shouting through the sheep as he came. The sheep scattered in all directions, their bells jangling. From the wild gesticulations and excited gruntings it became clear very quickly that Jo had missed something special. The Corporal confirmed it.

'It was a big one,' he said. 'I have never seen an eagle so big. He saw it first, didn't you, Hubert?' Hubert had the binoculars to his eyes and was pointing to the mountains. 'And I did not believe him,' the Corporal went on, 'not at first, because I could not see it. It was not in the air you see; it was on the ground. Perhaps it had just caught something, maybe it was a rabbit; and then it took off up into the air and we followed it.' He laughed. 'Hubert would not take the binoculars from his eyes and he kept tripping over, but we did not lose it. We followed it higher always higher, until it landed on a shelf of rock. And there were twigs there, I saw them. I think it must be a nest Jo.'

'Did you see any young birds?' Jo said.

The Corporal shook his head. 'Maybe we go back another day. Next Friday yes?'

'Maybe,' said Jo, shrugging his shoulders. He was doing his best to conceal his enthusiasm.

'Good,' said the Corporal. 'I shall look forward to it.'

Even after he had gone Hubert never stopped flying about like an eagle. As they drove the sheep back into the village that evening he was still at it, flapping his arms like wings, curling his hands into claws and shrieking. Jo found himself almost annoyed with Hubert for having enjoyed it so much. Eagle's nest or not, he would not go with the Corporal next Friday, he would not.

That Sunday after Mass Jo saw Father Lasalle talking earnestly to Grandpère and Lieutenant Weissmann outside the church door. At lunch Grandpère was unusually quiet – Maman noticed it too.

'Is there something the matter?' she said.

Grandpère pushed away his plate and lit a cigarette. 'That Boche Corporal, the big one,' he said, 'you know him? Well, he's just about the best of them I'd say.'

'What about him?' said Maman.

'He had three daughters,' Grandpère said, 'and now he's got two. One of them was killed in a bombing raid on Berlin last week.'

'Poor man,' said Maman. 'Poor man.'

Grandpère stood up, angry. 'Why poor man, eh? If he'd stayed at home and looked after his family like he should have done, like they all should have done, he'd still have three daughters, wouldn't he? And my son, your husband, wouldn't be shut up in some camp, and those children . . .' He stopped short and coughed.

Maman looked at him sharply. 'What children?' she asked, but Grandpère pretended not to have heard and by the time she asked again he was almost out of the room.

'I'm going up to the hut,' he said and he was gone.

'Why is Grandpère angry?' asked Christine.

'I don't know, dear,' said Maman still frowning after him. 'I don't know.'

The following Friday the mist was still lying in the valley when the Corporal came by as he'd promised he would. Jo half hoped that he wouldn't come for he knew that he would not be able to refuse him now, and that's how it turned out. The Corporal seemed a different man. All the jollity was gone, all the warmth. His eyes were red and vacant. 'You are coming, Jo?' he said, and he handed Jo the binoculars. Hubert wanted to come again but he was quite used to taking turns, and anyway the half bar of chocolate the Corporal offered seemed a tempting enough substitute. They left him guarding the sheep. When Jo looked back he was making Rouf lie down and beg for his chocolate.

They walked on without speaking. 'We won't be able to see much in the mist,' said Jo.

'When we get higher it will be better.'

It was several minutes before Jo found the courage to speak of it but he knew he had to. 'About what happened to your daughter,' he said. 'I'm sorry, everyone's sorry.'

'Thank you, Jo,' said the Corporal. 'Thank you.' And then he started talking and once he had started he didn't stop. 'If there has to be a war,' he said, 'then it should be fought between soldiers. Before, it was always between soldiers, that I can understand. I do not like it, but I can understand it. At Verdun it was one soldier in a uniform against another soldier in another uniform. What have women and children to do with the fighting of wars, tell me that? Every day since I hear about my daughter,

109

every day I ask myself many questions and I try to answer them. It is not so easy. What are we doing here, Wilhelm, I ask myself? Answer: I'm guarding the Frontier. Question: why? Answer: to stop people escaping. Question: why do they want to escape? Answer: because they are in fear of their lives. Question: who are these people? Answer: Frenchmen who do not want to be taken to work in Germany, maybe a few prisoners-of-war escaping, and Jews. Question: who is it that threatens the lives of Jews? Answer: we do. Question: why? Answer: There is no answer. Question: and when they are captured, what happens? Answer: concentration camp. Question: and then? Answer: no answer, not because there is no answer, Jo, but because we are frightened to know the answer.' He wiped his cheeks with the back of his hand and laughed. 'You see what happens when you ask so many questions, Jo? When I was little I always asked too many questions and my mother would become impatient. When I asked why again and again she would say, "a blue reason, Willi, a blue reason".' Jo smiled at that. 'So,' said the Corporal, 'we smile again. We must smile. It is good to smile. Now we look for eagles.'

As they climbed out of the trees they left the mist below them and reached a wide plain of spongy grass, dotted with grey-blue thistles and scattered rocks, with a silver stream running through it.

'It was here,' said the Corporal. 'We were here when we saw it last time.' He pointed upwards.

'Look, can you see there? Up there, half-way up the mountain. How do you say it, a ledge, yes? It was up there, I am sure of it.' Jo trained the binoculars on the rock face. 'Higher, a little higher, Jo. Can you see it?' And there it was, a wide ledge of rock, a dark recess behind it and at one end a nest of twigs, but no eagle.

'She's not there,' said Jo, 'and I can't see a chick.'

'She'll come,' said the Corporal, 'if she comes once then she'll come again. We must be patient. We will move higher up the mountain, that way we can see better.'

Jo followed him across the valley, leapt the stream and scrambled up the shale on hands and feet until they came to a steep slope that was always covered in blueberries in September. Jo had often been up there picking them with Papa. They squatted down in the shadow of a great rock. From there they could look back across the narrow valley and into the ledge.

The Corporal took the binoculars and trained them. 'Better,' he said, 'much better. Here she will not see us, but we will see her. Now we wait, we wait and pray.' Jo looked at him. 'Something is wrong?' asked the Corporal.

Jo turned away and shook his head. 'I know someone else who often says the same thing,' said Jo, 'that's all.'

'Here,' said the Corporal, 'you have the binoculars. Now we must be still. We must be silent.'

They sat side by side, knees drawn up, eyes scanning the sky about them. They spotted birds by the score, vultures, ravens, larks, buzzards and a lone red kite that absorbed them for an hour or more, but no eagle. Jo was training the binoculars on a vulture high above him, drawing it into focus until it filled the circle of the glass. He could see the feathers on it, how they wrapped around the wind and kept it floating up there. Suddenly the Corporal's arm was on his shoulder and squeezing him. Jo swung the glasses across to the ledge and caught up with the eagle just as she landed. She dropped something at her feet, Jo could not make out what it was. The eagle shook herself and surveyed the world beneath her, then she picked up her prey – it looked like a marmot Jo thought – and sidled along the ledge towards the nest. There she dropped it, stood a claw on it and began to pick at it. It was then that Jo saw something moving in the shadows under the rock behind her. A chick came lurching and hopping over the twigs towards the eagle.

'Look,' he whispered. 'Look.'

'Please?' said the Corporal holding out his hand, and Jo handed him the binoculars. '*Prima! Ausgezeichnet!*' murmured the Corporal. '*Ausgezeichnet*. I think there's two of them, Jo. Yes, there's two,' and he handed the binoculars back to Jo. Infuriatingly it took some time for Jo to find the ledge again and focus; but then he had them, all three of them, and he was watching an eagles' tea party of shredded marmot. They pulled at it, all of them, tearing at the same piece and hopping backwards until it snapped. Jo felt the Corporal tapping him on his arm but he was so entranced that he was reluctant to hand back the glasses. The tapping became more insistent. Jo lowered the glasses and made to hand them over but the Corporal didn't seem to want them. He was pointing down to the valley below them. Jo looked. Three soldiers were moving slowly towards the stream. He could hear their voices now. Jo turned his binoculars on them but before he could focus they had moved out of sight behind a large boulder. One by one they emerged the other side. Jo looked up at the Corporal who shrugged his shoulders and smiled. 'It's all right, Jo,' he said, 'I've got my papers.' Jo looked down at them again. Someone was moving through the trees beyond the boulder. Another soldier, Jo thought. He lifted the binoculars a fraction; it was no soldier. As Jo focused the binoculars his worst fears were realised. Benjamin was crouching now at the edge of the wood. He was looking this way and that, as if he was about to dash out across the open towards the cover of some nearby rocks, and Jo saw with a sickening heart that from where Benjamin was he could not possibly see the patrol behind the boulder. They only had to walk on a few more paces and he would come face to face with them.

Chapter Seven

The Corporal was on his feet, hands cupped to his mouth. 'Ola! Ola!' he shouted, and the echo resounded around the valley. The patrol stopped. 'Ola! Ola!' and he waved both arms in the air. The soldiers were looking about them in alarm, their rifles at the ready. The Corporal laughed and shook his head. 'I think it is Rudi's patrol,' he said. 'We call them "the grandfathers". They are even older than I am.' Jo looked beyond the boulder into the trees. Benjamin had vanished. One of the soldiers had seen them now and was pointing excitedly. 'Maybe we should go down to them,' said the Corporal, 'so that they can see who we are. We do not want them to think that we are escaping over the border, do we? Come on, Jo.' And he helped him to his feet. The soldiers were running up towards them. 'It's Rudi. No-one else runs like Rudi. You know what he is, Jo? He's, how do you say, a taxidermist. You know what they do? No? I tell you then. He is someone who stuffs dead animals, fish perhaps, birds even.' Jo was not listening. He was straining to find some movement amongst the trees beyond the boulder. There was none. Benjamin had gone. He was sure of it now. He was safe. Jo heard his heart pounding in his throat and swallowed to stop it. '*Was ist los?*' said the Corporal. 'Something is wrong, Jo?' Jo shook his head. 'You don't look so good.'

'I'm all right,' said Jo. 'I'm all right.' The Corporal took Jo by the elbow. 'Come, we go down. Poor old Rudi, it would give him a heart attack if we made him come all the way up here.'

There followed a laughing reunion half-way up the slope. Jo could not understand much of what they were saying but he could see that the Corporal was explaining all about the eagle's nest and by the way they looked at him all about Jo too. There was lots of nodding, lots of '*ja ja*'s and more laughing, and then as if to prove the point the eagle shrieked right above them, circled once and soared away over the peaks, the soldiers' binoculars trained on her. But Jo's eyes were still searching the trees. 'Quick Jo,' said the Corporal, 'you will miss it.' But in the time Jo took to lift the binoculars to his eyes and focus, the eagle had gone and the sky above the peaks was empty.

It was late afternoon before they rounded the bend in the track and saw Hubert sitting where they had left him on his rock. Rouf lifted his head off his lap and yawned. He stretched and came plodding towards them. Hubert didn't hear them until the sheep moved in closer together, then he turned and saw them. He was clearly more pleased to see the binoculars than anything else. In a trice he had them around his neck. The Corporal smiled and began to walk away.

'What about your binoculars?' Jo called after him.

He walked backwards for a few paces as he spoke. 'He can keep them. They make him happy, yes? And I have another pair, my army ones, much better, much stronger. Those are my own, yours now, Hubert. *Auf Wiedersehen.*'

It took some time for Hubert to believe that the binoculars were really his but when he did everyone in the village had to know and everyone had to look through them and share in his joy. He wore them around his neck constantly, even when he was milking the sheep. His father said he often slept with them on at night.

More than ever now the Corporal was held in genuine affection throughout the village, for the gift did not smack of bribery but of open generosity. His spirits seemed to recover quickly in this cocoon of warmth – perhaps a little too quickly some said, Madame Soulet for one; but Jo knew this not to be so.

The two of them, the Corporal and Jo, often sat for long hours together on the rock. They were not allowed up into the mountains again the Corporal told him – Lieutenant Weissmann had forbidden it. But anyway they were content to be where they were. They watched the sheep and the birds, and Jo felt the raw pain of grief in the Corporal's long silences. The Corporal never again spoke of his dead daughter, except once when he said it would be her birthday soon. It was that day that Hubert came stumbling along the track towards them, his binoculars around his neck as usual. He seemed unusually awkward and shy as he sat down beside Jo and rocked back and forth. He often seemed to do this when he was tense. Quite suddenly he stopped rocking and took a deep breath. He reached inside his shirt. Jo had expected him to produce a frog or a toad perhaps, but when his hand came out he was holding a packet of cigarettes. He reached across Jo and offered one to the Corporal.

The Corporal shook his head and smiled. 'No thank you, Hubert. Since the war began I smoke too much. In my letters I promise my wife not to smoke. If I promise then I can stop, you understand me, yes?' Hubert frowned and insisted, holding the packet closer to the Corporal. 'Very well, Hubert, just this once then,' he said, and he took the packet.

Hubert drew his knees up and rocked again. The Corporal opened the packet and when Jo saw the cotton wool he knew what it was all about. Hubert had his hands over his eyes as the Corporal tugged gently at the cotton wool until it came free. He seemed to guess now what it was and pulled away the cotton wool with the utmost care. It was a tiny white chalice, and as the Corporal turned it slowly in his hand on the bed of cotton wool Jo could see that around it flew two golden eagles, their spread wings touching.

'He makes them,' said Jo.

The Corporal nodded. 'I know,' he said, holding it up to the light. It was translucent. 'Hubert's father,' he went on, 'he showed me his collection.' He folded it in the cotton wool again and slipped it back inside the cigarette packet. He slipped down off the rock and stood in front of Hubert. He reached out and took Hubert's hands away from his face. He leaned forward and kissed Hubert on both cheeks, patted him on the knee and walked away.

'He liked it,' said Jo, but Hubert had spotted a limping sheep and was off after it, shadowing it with Rouf into a corner of the field until they had it boxed in. He caught it by the back leg, picked something out of the foot, smacked its bottom and sent it bleating on its way.

They brought the sheep back in early that day because it was coming on to rain. Everyone else had the same idea so there was a muddle of sheep in the narrow village streets before they managed to drive them at last into the walled yard in front of the house. Jo thought he was a few sheep short and was counting them when Grandpère came to the door and called him in. Something was up, he could see it in his face. The sheep moved aside as he walked through them. Grandpère stood on the doorstep, a

118

cigarette hanging between his lips.

'Is it the children?' Jo spoke softly.

'Nothing like that,' said Grandpère throwing away his cigarette. 'Indoors, I've got something to show you.'

'What about the milking?'

'The sheep can wait, Jo,' he said. 'Come on,' and he took his arm.

As Jo went into the kitchen his suspicions were confirmed. Something *was* wrong. Christine was sitting silently on her mother's lap. Christine never sat on anyone's lap and was never quiet. She was staring across the room. Maman rested her chin on Christine's head. There were tears in her eyes. 'Jo,' she said, and then Jo saw the man standing by the window. The stranger had his back to him, his hands deep in the pockets of a long, dirty coat. As he turned round the evening light fell across his face and Jo saw at once it was his father. It was not the father he remembered from nearly four years before, but a smaller man, a thinner man, whose hair was no longer black but quite grey, and when Jo hugged him he could feel the sharp shoulder blades through his coat.

'Let me look at you, Jo,' said Papa, and he held him at arm's length. 'You've grown,' he said. The skin was stretched like paper over his cheekbones. 'Not that bad is it, Jo? You do recognise me, don't you?'

'Of course, Papa,' said Jo.

'More than your sister did. Still, that's not her

fault is it? She was no more than a babe when I left.'

'They let him out, Jo,' said Grandpère. 'Sent him home.'

'Don't go thinking it was out of the kindness of their hearts,' said Papa. 'They'd had all of me they wanted, used me all up.' Jo turned to his mother for an explanation.

'Papa's sick, Jo. Tuberculosis,' she said. 'They sent him home because he couldn't work any more.'

'It was the damp,' said Papa. 'There were dozens of us like it. No use to them any more. So they sent us home. You know Michel, Michel Maurois? They sent us back together, him and me. He's not grumbling, and neither am I, I can tell you. What's a bit of a wheezy chest when it's a passport home. Just give me a week or two and I'll be right as rain.'

They sat long together over supper that evening while Papa tried to catch up on the years he'd missed, and as the hours passed Christine ventured closer and closer to him. By the time she was taken up to bed she let him kiss her goodnight.

'That's the best thing that's happened to me in a long time,' he said.

Grandpère tried to ask about the prison camp but Papa would say nothing about it except to say that 'you learn things about yourself you never wanted to know'. There were long silences when he seemed to drift away into a world of his own. A mere mention of the soldiers in the village made him immediately angry and even the subject of Grandpère's pigs seemed to irritate him. Until he asked after the sheep Maman had said very little.

'Jo stepped right into your shoes,' she said, and Jo saw Papa's face darken suddenly. 'I told you in my letters, didn't I?' she went on. 'You'd have been proud of him. Maybe he missed school more often than he should but Monsieur Audap understood. Thinks very highly of our Jo does Monsieur Audap.'

'Monsieur Audap?' said Papa.

'His teacher,' she said. 'Don't you remember?'

'Oh yes,' said Papa and he looked away. He seemed to have forgotten so much about the village, about everything, and Jo could see that it hurt him to know it and to know that others knew it. Jo wished Maman would stop talking about how useful he'd been. Every word she spoke seemed to shrivel Papa up, but still she went on. 'Hubert helped him of course. We couldn't have managed without him. You remember Hubert?'

'Of course,' Papa snapped. 'Of course I do.'

Grandpère tried to make light of it. 'And me,' he said. 'What about me? Did I sit on my backside for four years, eh? Who took the sheep up onto the summer pastures? I did. Who moved the sheep when he was at school, eh? I did. Your old father, that's who.' He got up and poured Papa some more wine. 'And now you're back again I can hang up my boots.'

'Not yet you can't,' said Maman. 'We've got to get him well first. Good food and a warm house and plenty of rest. That's what he needs.'

'Don't fuss me,' said Papa, and he drank down his wine as if he hated it.

Grandpère leaned forward and tapped his knee. 'I've been courting, son,' he said, and Papa's laughter filled the house for the first time.

'It's true,' said Maman, 'everyone knows it. He's up and down to that old woman's house. Talk of the village it is.'

'What old woman?' Papa asked.

'Widow Horcada,' said Maman, 'the Black Widow.'

'You're not serious?' Papa was still laughing.

'And why not?' said Grandpère in mock indignation. 'Cleverest woman in the parish. She never parts with a penny she doesn't have to. She even pays Jo with honey doesn't she Jo?'

'What for?'

'For carrying her shopping,' said Grandpère.

Jo sat in silent admiration. In a few moments he had cheered Papa and explained in advance all the comings and goings to and from the Widow Horcada's house. Papa was still chuckling as he got up.

'I can see I came back just in time to stop my father from making an old fool of himself.'

'Too late for that, son,' he said. 'I'm a smitten man and there's nothing you nor anyone can do about it.'

Papa was putting on his coat.

'Where are you going?' Maman said.

'Out,' he said. 'You know, whilst I was in the

camp I looked forward to a lot of things, to seeing you, to being home again.' He frowned suddenly. 'You won't believe this,' he said, 'but sometimes I even forgot what you all looked like, all except Rouf there. And you can't look forward to what you can't remember. What I wanted to do most was to walk the hills at night, to feel alive again, to feel free. So that's what I'm going to do.'

They looked at each other frantically as he walked towards the door. 'But you can't,' said Maman. 'You're tired. You're not well. You'll catch a chill.'

'I'll be all right,' he said, opening the door. 'I won't be long.'

Grandpère was beside him. He took his arm and shut the door firmly. 'You can't go out,' he said. 'There's a curfew.'

'Curfew?'

'After nine thirty. If the Boche catch you outside after nine thirty . . .'

'What'll they do?' said Papa, the fury rising in his voice. 'Put me in prison? Shoot me? Let them. I've been shut up for four years and now I'm home I'm not letting any Boche make a prisoner of me in my own home. I'll come and I'll go as I please. Now out of my way, Papa. Out of my way!' Grandpère stood aside and Papa opened the door, pulled up his collar and walked out into the darkness.

They sat up and waited for him, dreading the sound of running boots, of shouting voices or even a volley of shots. The longer they waited the more terrible their fears became. When he did come back an hour or so later, all he said was: 'I saw them but they didn't see me.' The walk seemed to have dissipated the anger in him.

Jo lay in bed and listened to the murmur of voices from his parents' room next door. Papa really was back home. The last few hours had been no dream. Then came the coughing, fits of coughing followed by silences long enough to let Jo drift into sleep before the next fit began. But the coughing woke Christine and she was up and down the passage all night. Jo gave up all attempts to sleep and waited for the first sound of the dawn chorus.

The next day the village was alive with new joy and hope. No-one doubted that the war was being won; it was only a question of time now, that was all. Two of their sons had been returned to them, good enough cause for celebration. In such times any excuse for celebration was seized upon eagerly. Hubert was sent beating his drum around the village, his binoculars still around his neck, and everyone gathered in the Square to hear the Mayor's formal welcome. Papa and Michel Maurois stood either side of him, but Jo thought they endured rather than enjoyed the speech. It finished with a typical flourish. 'We await the day,' said Monsieur Sarthol, 'and it will surely not now be long, when the rest of our fathers and brothers, our uncles and nephews are returned to us once again. *Vive la France!*' Jo looked about him as everyone clapped and cheered and laughed – there wasn't a soldier in sight.

When Jo arrived at school the next morning they crowded around him to congratulate him. He was not sure what he had done to deserve it all, but he enjoyed it just the same. Not everyone, though, wanted to share in the general rejoicing. There were baleful, even resentful looks from across the playground, reminding Jo that many of the children still had fathers in prisoner-of-war camps. Laurent seemed to bear him no grudge, but then Laurent was not like that, and besides he had his reasons. 'I can't stand my father anyway,' he said, 'and neither can my mother. The longer they keep him there the better.' Laurent always said exactly what he thought however it reflected on him, and Jo admired that in him; but now it made Jo feel even more of a fraud. Papa was back home and Jo wished he wasn't. That was the truth of it. No matter how hard he tried to feel differently, he could not. Papa was a stranger to him and not a particularly welcome one either. It wasn't that he hated him, he just did not know him any more.

On Sunday Father Lasalle played a thundering triumphal march on the organ, and thanked God for their deliverance. That evening Jo was in the café when Papa and Michel got up and danced together on the table. The dancing spread out into the Square. Monsieur Audap sang songs nobody thought he ought to know and Hubert wrapped himself in the bearskin from the wall and ran growling and roaring after the children through the streets.

When the Corporal and two other soldiers walked into the café no-one took a blind bit of notice. The Corporal nodded and smiled at Jo as he sat down at the table in the corner. Jo smiled back. Suddenly Papa was on his feet, kicking his chair back against the wall. The awful silence was punctuated by distant roars and shrieks out in the Square. Michel tried to hold him back but Papa would not be stopped. He shook himself free, glaring at the three soldiers.

Grandpère stood up beside him. 'Let's go home,' he said.

'Not just yet,' said Papa, and then in a loud voice, 'Well, well. Look what's come to welcome us home, Michel.' He picked up a bottle and walked across the room towards where the soldiers were sitting. '*Guten Abend*,' he said, the sneer quite evident in his tone.

'Good evening,' said the Corporal without looking up.

'You must join our little party,' said Papa, his voice heavy and slurred with drink. He poured wine into each of their glasses.

Grandpère was trying to pull him away. 'That's enough,' he said. 'Come on, come home.' But Papa ignored him.

'There,' he said, 'some good French wine.' He raised the bottle in the air. 'To victory,' he said.

The soldiers sat, heads bowed, motionless. Then the Corporal stood up and he faced Papa, his glass in his hand. 'I drink to peace,' he said and he drank down his glass and put it on the table.

At that moment Hubert appeared at the door, the bearskin draped over his head and Laurent clutching an arm. Hubert beamed at the Corporal. Papa reached out and caught the swinging binoculars around Hubert's neck. 'Nice,' he said. Hubert laughed and put them to his eyes. He scanned the room until he focused on a stuffed buzzard on a shelf above the bar. He pointed at it. 'Bang!' he said. 'Bang! Bang!' and he laughed and then everyone laughed and was glad of it.

'They're his,' said Laurent. 'The Corporal gave them to you, didn't he, Hubert? You can see anything. I've seen the mountains on the moon.'

'Have you?' said Papa acidly. 'So now we accept presents from them do we?' Jo ran over to him. He had to explain. Papa had to know about the Corporal, about how kind he had been, about what happened to his daughter.

'Papa,' he said, touching his arm.

Papa turned on him, eyes full of fury. 'So he's a friend of yours too, is he?' Jo backed away.

The Corporal picked up his cap from the table. 'Good night,' he said and he passed Hubert on the way out putting a hand on his shoulder. The two soldiers followed him. Papa began to cough violently until he was doubled up. Grandpère took the bottle out of his hand and put an arm around him.

'We'll get him home, Jo,' he said.

In the weeks that followed Papa took very little interest in the farm or in anything else much. He tramped the hillsides all day to return each evening grim and sullen. The evenings he would spend with Michel in the café and Grandpère would go with him to be sure of getting him back before curfew, and when he did come back he was always drunk. Jo remembered him coming home drunk before he went away to the war but then he'd come back happy with the world and singing, now he would sit by the stove and brood darkly. Jo did not even dare to catch his eye for fear of encountering the look of accusing disapproval that he felt was following him wherever he went. The father he'd grown up with, with whom he'd shared the shepherd's hut all summer long, was not the man now sharing his house. They had a stranger living with them and all of them knew it.

Once Jo had come home to find Maman crying in the kitchen. Jo put his arms around her but could not find the words to comfort her. Grandpère did better. 'He'll come out of it, Lise,' he said, 'you'll see. You've got to put yourself in his place. It's like he's come back from the dead – that's what it's like for him. He comes back home expecting everything to be the same and it isn't. You're not the same. I'm not the same. Jo here has grown as tall as he is. There's a lot of bitterness in him, Lise, a lot of poison; but it'll come to a head and then he'll be free of it. Just give him time.' But time seemed only to make matters worse. Even Grandpère's valiant efforts to cheer him fell on deaf ears.

For both of them the journeys up to the children's cave with supplies brought welcome relief. Jo would often go off into the forest with Benjamin to gather firewood. They would talk of the bear and wonder together how big it must be by now and where it was living. And Grandpère would tell his troubles to Widow Horcada who never seemed that sympathetic.

One afternoon they were on their way back home from the cave when Hubert came running up to them pointing behind him into the bracken and grunting with excitement. He took off his binoculars and handed them to Jo. All Jo could see at first was Rouf's tail, and then a wild boar charged out of the bracken and across the field. Hubert went galloping after him. The last they saw of him he was bounding into the bracken, a stick in his hand, and shouting 'Bang! Bang!' They laughed and turned for home.

Papa was sitting alone in the kitchen. He looked up as they came in. He had a glass of wine in his hand. 'Where've you been?' he said. A frown came across his face as he caught sight of the binoculars. He stood up and lunged for Jo, catching him by the straps of the binoculars. 'What's this then?' Until that moment Jo had forgotten he still had them.

'Hubert's binoculars, Papa. He lent them to me. We saw this boar, didn't we Grandpère?'

'I've been hearing things I don't like, Jo,' said Papa, pulling him closer. Jo could smell the drink on his breath. He tried to pull away but found himself held fast.

'Leave him be,' said Grandpère.

'You stay out of this,' said Papa. 'He's my son. You and her, you've done enough harm as it is. Only four years I've been gone and look what you've turned him into.'

'What do you mean, Papa?' said Jo.

'Collaborator, that's what I mean.' Jo shook his head. 'I've been told so don't you go denying it. You went off with that Boche Corporal didn't you?'

'I was only watching the eagles.'

'Damn you! Don't lie to me!' The blow came without warning and sent Jo reeling backwards into Grandpère who staggered but held him upright. Jo put his hand on his cheek. He could not feel it. He licked his lip and tasted blood. Grandpère stepped in front of him as Maman came running in. She rushed over to him.

'What've you done?' she cried.

Grandpère sat Jo down in a chair. 'He'll be all right,' he said.

'How could you?' she said. 'He's your own son. What's happened to you? What did they do to you in that camp?'

'You want to know what happened?' Papa was breathing hard. 'I'll tell you what happened. They gutted me like a fish. Don't you understand? They took away four years of my life that's what they did. And when I come back, what do I find, eh? The whole lousy village playing lovey-dovey with them and my own son making friends with the filthy Boche. That's what they are, don't you know what they are? Don't you know what they've done?'

'We had to live,' said Maman reaching for his hand and holding on to it when he tried to pull away from her.

He was crying openly now. 'My own son a collaborator. Do you know what those binoculars are? They're a badge of shame. Hubert's a halfwit. You can't blame him; but my son, my own son . . .' And he could say no more.

Grandpère pulled a handkerchief out of his pocket and gave it to Jo. 'Here,' he said, 'we don't want blood everywhere do we?' He knocked a cigarette out of a packet and offered one to Papa who shook his head. 'Sit him down, Lise,' said Grandpère firmly, 'and give him a brandy.' She led Papa to a chair. 'And I'll have one too. We'll all have one, to celebrate. You don't know what we're celebrating do you? Well, I'll tell you, but you won't like it. I haven't talked to you like this since you were a little boy and I shouldn't be doing it now in front of Jo, but I'm going to do it anyway.' Grandpère took his brandy. 'Sit down, Lise. You'd better hear this too. You won't like it much either but for a different reason perhaps. Let me tell you something about this boy of yours, this "collaborator" as you call him.'

Jo knew what he was going to say. 'Don't Grandpère,' he said. 'You mustn't.'

'Yes I must, Jo,' he said. 'I'll not have him

thinking of you like that, nor of me, nor of any of us.' He turned back to Papa. 'This boy of yours may not look like much, doesn't make a lot of noise, he just goes on quietly; but I'll tell you something for nothing. Single-handed, until just a few months back, single-handed mind you, this boy has been taking Widow Horcada's supplies up and down the mountain. Not much in that, you'd say; but do you know who it's really all been for? Well, I'll tell you then. There's twelve children – Jews – hiding away in a cave up in the forest, waiting to be taken over into Spain. Some of them have been waiting for near enough two years, and all that time they've needed feeding and all that time your Jo's been doing it. Without that boy of yours, that "collaborator", they'd not have stood a chance. He's kept them alive and he's kept his mouth shut.' Maman had her hand to her mouth. 'He couldn't have told you, Lise, he couldn't have. He'd given his word, and anyway you'd have only tried to stop him.' He turned back to Papa. 'Now, you may not know it where you've been hidden away, but there's a law hereabouts, laid down by our Boche friends, and it's this: anyone who's caught aiding or abetting the escape of fugitives will be shot. Jo's known that all the time he's been doing it. Every day of his life your son could have been taken out and shot.'

As Jo listened he was suddenly terrified, retrospectively terrified. Of course he'd known it but he'd not thought about it, not properly. It had never sunk in until now. It was as if Grandpère had been talking about someone else. There had been no real intention on his part. Things had just happened. When Grandpère had finished he looked at Papa. He was leaning forward, his head in his hands.

'Jo,' he said, 'what have I done to you? What've I said?'

'Nothing that can't be undone,' said Grandpère. 'Nothing that can't be unsaid. On your feet the two of you,' and he drew them together.

After they hugged, Papa held Jo by the shoulders, and smiled through his tears. 'You're taller than me,' he said, and he turned away. 'The children,' he went on. 'They're still up there then, up in the cave?'

'Still up there,' said Grandpère, and he told him all about Benjamin and Widow Horcada, and how they were waiting for the right moment to take the children over the mountains.

Papa walked to the mantlepiece and leant on it for a moment. Then he turned round. 'You're crazy, crazy,' he said. 'At any moment a patrol could stumble across that cave. What have you been waiting for – a miracle? For the war to end? For the Boche to fall asleep?'

'I told you,' said Grandpère, 'there's patrols out everywhere. Benjamin's seen them. I've seen them, and besides some of the children have been too weak to move.'

'Weak or not,' said Papa vehemently, 'they've got

to go. If necessary they'll have to be carried, but they've got to go.'

'Just tell us how,' said Grandpère. 'You tell us how to do it and we'll do it. Don't you think we haven't thought about it?' Papa said nothing.

'Maybe,' said Maman quietly, 'maybe the children could pretend to be someone they weren't.'

'What do you mean?' Grandpère said.

'I don't know,' she said, 'I was just thinking aloud really. But I remember when I was little I was told some story about a one-eyed giant, and there were all these men in a cave and a giant was waiting outside to kill them as they came out, and there were some sheep sheltering inside the cave with them.'

'I know it, I remember it,' said Papa, and he went on. 'When the sheep come out of the cave they're all clinging on underneath and he doesn't see them. You're not suggesting . . .'

'No, of course I'm not,' said Maman, 'but sheep need shepherds don't they? It's been a warm Spring. There'll be plenty of grass by now on the high pastures. By my reckoning there must be two thousand sheep in the village, a hundred cows or more, fifty horses maybe, and your pigs too, Grandpère. When the time's right, and after all we can choose when the time's right, they'll all be moving up into the mountains for the Summer won't they? No-one will notice a few more children shepherding them will they? And once you get up to the hut, well, it's like you always say, Grandpère, you're so close to Spain up there you could almost spit into it.' They all looked at her. 'Just an idea,' she said.

Chapter Eight

It was strange seeing Widow Horcada sitting in their kitchen with Grandpère fussing around her. She and Maman were polite to each other but no more than that. She listened intently as Papa told her the plan. When it was over she sat back in her chair and wrinkled her nose. 'I don't know,' she said. 'I don't know. It seems to me the more people you tell the greater the risk that someone will talk, and you want to tell everyone.'

'But don't you see, Alice,' said Grandpère, 'everyone has to know, we need them to know, else they won't all come to the concert will they? And how else are we going to find enough clothes for the children, eh? Then we've got to find a place for them to sleep the night before and a family to look after them on the way up to the hut; and they've all got to act like they know the children. It just won't work unless everyone knows.'

'I know all that,' said the Widow. 'But can they all be trusted? Can you be sure of them, of every one of them? Madame Soulet? Armand Jollet?' No-one answered. She went on. 'All you need is one of them to take fright, and after all, they'll know what'll happen to them if they're caught.'

'You knew,' said Maman quickly, 'and so did Jo and so did Grandpère. It didn't stop any of you doing what was right, did it?' The Widow looked at her sharply. 'No-one's going to give them away,' Maman went on, 'because if they did they'd know it wouldn't be just the children in the cave who would suffer, it would be all of us – the whole of the village, everyone they've grown up with, all of us.'

'That's the beauty of it, Alice,' said Grandpère. 'Don't you see? We're all in it together, sink or swim. That's why everyone has to be part of it; and they'll want to be too when they hear about the children. There's some good folk in this village and they'll bring the others along with them.'

'They'll be frightened,' said Maman, 'like I was when Grandpère told me all about Jo and you and those children up in the cave; and I'll tell you something else, I'm still frightened, but I know it has to be done and so will they. They'll do it, you'll see.'

Widow Horcada smiled at Maman and chuckled. 'You've got some spirit in you, girl,' she said, 'more than you ever let on, eh?' Jo had never heard his mother so forthright, so determined.

'Well,' Papa said. 'Do we do it or don't we? We

can't stay talking about it for ever.'

The Widow Horcada looked at him steadily and took a deep breath. 'We do it,' she said, 'and may God help us.'

'Amen,' said Grandpère.

They spent the next hour or so compiling a list of names. 'We've got to see every single one of them,' said Papa. 'Monsieur Sarthol first, then Father Lasalle. If he won't help us out with the concert, then we'll have to call it off anyway; and then Monsieur Audap to see if he'll let the children off school on Monday. We need the children, more than anyone we need the children, all of them.'

* * *

Father Lasalle announced the concert during Mass. Everyone had been told about it by now and was expecting it, except for the soldiers of course. Looking directly at Lieutenant Weissmann and the dozen or so soldiers sitting with him Father Lasalle spoke with his usual intoning drone but also with the authority of a man who was used to commanding attention. 'For three months every summer,' he said, 'our small community loses many of its men folk. As we all know, on Monday next begins the great exodus, the transhumance, the beginning of months of solitude and hard work. In Lescun it has always been thus. Now I have lived here amongst you for most of my life, long enough to know that some of these men might want to spend their last evening in the café, and that is something I would not wish to deny them even if I could. So by all means go to the café; but I want everyone, and I do mean everyone, to come here to the church afterwards.' Jo was looking along the pew towards the soldiers; he wanted to watch their faces for any flicker of disbelief. The Corporal leaned forward and winked at him and Jo looked away quickly.

'Vanity, vanity saith the preacher, all is vanity,' said Father Lasalle smiling broadly and putting his hand on his heart, 'and I confess freely to a great vanity. As you know, for many long hours I sit alone at the organ here in the church and I practise. I have been practising some of the greatest organ music ever written and it was written by a German too, one Johann Sebastian Bach. But for a musician practise is not enough. I must perform. My music must be heard. From time to time in the past I have given recitals and so tonight, to mark the eve of the transhumance I will be giving you one of my short concerts, and I want all of you here, a gathering of the entire community, every man, woman and child. No child is ever too young for Bach.' He leaned forward over the pulpit, his eyes raking the pews, his finger pointing. 'And you can be sure I shall know if you're not here.' There was some laughter at that. And then he spoke directly to Lieutenant Weissmann. 'The music, as I have said, will be German, Lieutenant. I know how fond you are of Bach and since it was written to glorify the God of both our peoples, you and your men will be most welcome. Catholic and Protestant, all will be welcome. Indeed, Lieutenant, I will be most disappointed if the entire German garrison is not here. Can I count on you, Lieutenant?' The Lieutenant nodded, smiling. 'That is kind of you, Lieutenant. I shall reserve seats for you. The concert will begin at eight o'clock and so it should be over well before curfew.' It was a masterly performance.

Father Lasalle's concerts were rarely well attended. That evening though the church was as full as Jo had ever seen it. But by five to eight the German soldiers had still not arrived. Jo sat next to Maman, her hand squeezing his. He squeezed back to reassure and be reassured. They would come, they had to come. Christine sat on the other side of her, thumb in her mouth, her legs swinging. The church was silent with expectation, not a murmur, not a cough. Jo turned and craned his neck. Still nothing. Maman pulled on his hand and he turned back again. The bells groaned in the tower and struck eight o'clock. Father Lasalle emerged from the vestry and looked at the empty pews where the soldiers should have been. He seemed uncertain what to do. At that moment the Lieutenant strode in, cap under his arm, the soldiers trooping in behind him. The sigh of relief was almost audible. Jo counted them in as Father Lasalle took his seat at the organ. Twenty-two. They were all there. Last to take their seats were the Mayor and Hubert. As they sat down in front of Jo he heard the doors close behind him.

The first piping notes sounded out through the church. Jo shivered, whether through pleasure or relief he did not know. From where he sat he could just see Father Lasalle's head rocking back and forth and the back of his heels stepping neatly across the foot pedals. Even the smallest children, Christine amongst them, were immediately absorbed in the music. Hubert was lost in it, his mouth open, his head nodding, but Jo found he could not keep his eye off the clock. He knew they needed at least an hour to be sure, an hour without soldiers in the streets, a clear hour to bring the children down from the cave and to hide them away in their allotted houses. Jo ventured a look at the Corporal. He was gazing up at the roof and his fingers were tapping out the rhythm on his knees.

At long last nine o'clock struck in horrible disharmony with the organ. Father Lasalle played on. There was a certain amount of shuffling and coughing now as people became more uncomfortable and the music too repetitive to hold their attention. Jo glanced across at Lieutenant Weissmann who was looking at his watch and whispering to the Corporal beside him. The Corporal shrugged his shoulders and smiled and then took out his handkerchief and blew his nose noisily. 'Keep going, Father,' Jo said to himself. 'Keep going, keep going.'

Hubert was fidgetting now and looking around the church through his binoculars until his father put a firm hand on his wrist and pulled his arm downwards. Hubert was not so easily deterred. Much to everyone's amusement he trained his binoculars on Father Lasalle and then on each of the soldiers in turn.

It was not far short of half past nine when the music built to a final crescendo leaving the church filled with a throbbing silence. The Mayor and Hubert led the enthusiastic applause and Father Lasalle came out to take his bows. He held up his hands and shrugged his shoulders. 'I'm afraid it lasted a little longer than I expected,' he said. 'Good night and God bless you.' Lieutenant Weissmann shook his hand and then came over to talk to the Mayor who nodded and turned to the audience. 'Ladies and gentlemen,' he announced. 'The Lieutenant has asked me to say that curfew is extended by half an hour tonight to allow us to get home at our ease. He asks us all to be home by ten o'clock.'

Jo danced his way through the crowd outside the porch and ran all the way home. He found Papa and Grandpère sitting at the kitchen table. Grandpère was pouring wine. 'Are they here?' he said.

'Up in the hayloft,' said Grandpère, 'all three of them.'

'Did you get them all?' said Jo.

'All of them,' said Papa, 'and they're all where they should be. We did it in under the hour.'

Jo climbed the ladder at the back of the barn and pushed open the loft door. 'Jo?' It was Benjamin's

142

voice whispering out of the darkness. 'Is that you, Jo?'

'It's me,' he said, and he hauled himself up into the loft.

'Léah's fast asleep,' said Benjamin, and in the darkness Jo could just make her out curled up tight against him, an arm thrown around his knee.

'I'm not.' It was Michael crawling towards them through the hay. 'Here,' he said. 'I brought you this.' He was trying to thrust something into Jo's hand. 'It's something you always wanted,' he said. 'Something you could never win. Squeeze it,' he said, 'and it'll bring you luck.' It was a chess piece, a white queen.

'I've told him, Jo,' said Benjamin. 'I've told him that for tomorrow he's your brother. And do you know what he told me, this horrible boy, he said if you were his brother he'd have taught you to play chess a lot better than you do.'

And then Jo saw Benjamin's face silhouetted for a moment against the window behind him. 'You cut your beard off,' said Jo.

'Your father's orders.' Benjamin stroked his chin. 'If you want to be taken for a native, he said, then you've got to look like one. It seems there's not many people round here with a red beard, so off it had to come. I feel a bit naked without it, a bit cold too. Still, it'll grow again. It had better do, hadn't it, or Anya won't recognise me when she sees me.'

'You're staying behind then,' said Jo.

'Yes,' said Benjamin. 'I'll see them safely over the

border and then I'll come back.' He put his arm around him. 'Jo,' he said, 'I feel surer than ever that somehow Anya will find her way here. You remember what I said to you a while back when I hurt my ankle, when the snows came and it all looked hopeless? You remember what I said? I said "Wait and pray". Well we waited and we prayed and here we are. This time tomorrow, God willing, the children will be in Spain and they'll be safe at last. So I shall wait up in the cave for Anya, and I shall pray.'

When Jo went down to the kitchen they were all there and Papa was crouching down in front of Christine and holding her hands. There was an edge of impatience in his voice. 'Forget about the donkey, Christine, just remember – stay with Jo. You clap your hands when he does, and you chase the sheep like Rouf does, and if anyone asks you've got a big sister called Léah and a big brother called Michael. Do you understand now?'

'But I haven't got a big sister,' she said, 'and my big brother's called Jo.'

Papa gave up and Maman took his place. 'It's pretend, Christine,' she said. 'Just for tomorrow you've got a pretend sister and she's called Léah and you've got a pretend brother and he's called Michael and you've got to look after them, no squabbling.'

'But can I ride the donkey?' she said and everyone had to laugh.

When she'd gone up to bed Papa stretched out in

his chair and Grandpère lit his last cigarette of the day – he always had a 'last one', usually several of them, before he went to bed. 'Some people,' he said, 'are so predictable. You know what Armand Jollet said when I told him? He said he ought to be compensated – compensated! You know what he said? He said, "if I go with you I'll have to close up the shop for a whole day and that'll cost me", and his chins shook like an agitated turkey. You should've seen him.'

'Money,' said Maman, 'it's all that man ever thinks of.'

'I've never really talked much to the schoolmaster, that Monsieur Audap,' said Papa. 'Always thought he was a strange fish. But he's not. He's a fine man. When I told him all about it and asked him about giving the children a day off school, he thought for a moment and I was sure he was going to refuse. He always looks such a miserable old so-and-so. Do you know what he said, Jo? He said the children would likely learn more in that one day than he could teach them in a lifetime. "Nothing's important unless it stays with you," that's what he said; "and no matter what happens, none of us," he said, "none of us is ever likely to forget tomorrow".'

Jo did not even try to sleep that night, he knew it would be pointless. His mind went over the plan again and again. He tried to visualise it as the soldiers would see it. Would it all look normal to them? Would they notice all the extra children in amongst the animals? Would they catch a glimpse of Benjamin's face and know him for a stranger? He could almost convince himself that it was going to work, that the Germans would see only what they were supposed to see: but as the night wore on a terrible doubt kept recurring. It was something the Corporal had told him a long time ago. He'd come from a village in the mountains, in Bavaria, 'just like Lescun,' he'd said. Well, Jo thought, if it was a lot like Lescun then he'd know that you don't need dozens and dozens of children to drive the animals, he'd know you can do the job with a few men and a couple of dogs and he'd know too that the flocks and herds were moved out separately and not in one great, chaotic bunch. The more Jo saw it through the Corporal's eyes the more he worried, and by dawn a multitude of nagging doubts had eclipsed his hopes. He faced the day ahead with a deep dread welling inside him.

At breakfast he recognised the same anxiety in Maman's eyes. Papa and Grandpère were still arguing on and on about who would be best to stay with the children in the hut and guide them over the mountains. Grandpère said that he was fitter, that Papa's coughing could give them away. Papa said he was younger and that anyway he knew the mountains better. At one point they were going to do it together, but Maman would have none of that. She said it was silly for two of them to take the risk of getting caught. In the end it was Papa who had his way.

Léah and Michael looked awkward in their country clothes. They ate ravenously and in silence. Christine just stared at them and refused to eat her breakfast. 'Time to go, I think,' said Papa. Benjamin finished his coffee and stood up.

'Monsieur, Madame,' he said, 'I hardly know you, but before we leave I want to thank you and through you all the people of this village for what you have done and what you are about to do. What has happened here in this little place, whether it succeeds or whether it fails, is evidence enough, if any were needed, that no-one will ever suppress the power for good, for compassion in the hearts of men and women. I have one regret though, that my little Anya is not yet here. But when she comes I shall tell her, I shall tell her often so that she can tell her children. Such things should not be forgotten. And now if you will allow me I will say a prayer. It is the last prayer we Jews say before we leave the Synagogue.' He closed his eyes. 'And the Lord shall be king over all the earth. In that day shall the Lord be one and His name be one.'

Rouf lay stretched out like a carpet by the stove with Léah crouched beside him stroking the top of his head. She leaned over and kissed him.

'Jo,' said Papa. 'You'd better wake that dog up. We can't move those sheep without him.' Jo whistled and Rouf woke, a look of resignation on his face. He yawned noisily and Léah laughed and sat back on her haunches as he stretched, shook himself awake, and then led them outdoors into the yard.

The streets were already full of sheep noise, a cacophony of bells and bleating and, claiming a bass line in the raucous choir, the cows bellowed and the donkeys brayed. The first flock came past them, Laurent driving them with his stick. He was leading a heavily laden donkey that stepped daintily over the cobbles. He winked at Jo as he passed and grinned. He was enjoying every minute of it. He had two of the cave children with him. They looked for all the world just like the village children around them. Like them they carried switches and sticks, like them they whistled and shouted and clapped. Two more flocks and a herd of cows came by, and Jo counted at least another five children from the cave.

Now it was their turn. Hubert was sitting on the wall laughing and pointing as they gathered up the sheep in the yard. Jo shouted to him to open the gate and he began to flap his arms and whistle. Michael followed his example at once with uninhibited enthusiasm. When Benjamin too turned shepherd Léah seemed to warm to the idea and joined in as well. As he left the yard Jo turned and waved to Grandpère and Papa – they'd be coming on behind with the pigs and the donkey.

By the time they reached the Square Jo saw that the flocks had bunched together and every street leading into it was thick with sheep and cattle. The noise was deafening, an incessant chorus of animals punctuated with whooping and whistling and barking. Jo saw a sheep burst through the front door of Monsieur Sarthol's house, a dog went in after it. Jo never saw what happened for his eye was taken by something far more worrying. Three soldiers, one of them the Corporal, were standing on top of the wall by the war memorial and watching everything that passed through the Square below them. Jo looked away quickly and whooped even louder at the sheep. A cow was rubbing itself against the corner of the café and the soldiers were laughing. Benjamin was keeping his head down as Papa had suggested he should, but to Jo his shepherding looked somehow forced and stiff. And then he felt Léah clutching his arm. She had seen the soldiers and was looking up at them, her eyes wide with terror. The Corporal was looking right at her and the sheep would not move on. There was nothing Jo could do. There were sheep behind him, sheep in front of him, sheep all about him. The Corporal had let himself down off the wall and was scrutinising them closely. He had noticed something – Jo was sure of it.

Why Hubert chose that moment to perform Jo never knew but he pushed his way through the sheep and began to leap up and down like a wild thing; and then raising his arms in the air he growled at the sheep like a bear. The Corporal pointed and laughed and the other soldiers laughed with him. Hubert saw it and performed his bear act again, but with redoubled vigour. All around him the sheep panicked. They pushed and shoved and jumped over each other and at last the great flock began to move again up past the baker's shop. Jo slipped around the back of Léah, ostensibly to chase a sheep, but this way he'd be between her and the soldiers so that she could not see them and they could not see her. He dared not venture another look at the soldiers until they'd left the Square behind them. When he did turn round the Corporal was looking straight at him. Jo turned away quickly and played shepherd again.

So the chaotic cavalcade wound its way slowly out of the village and up towards the hills beyond. They could see the circle of mountains ahead of them. All around him Jo could see and feel the exhilaration and relief. The ruse had surely worked. The cave children had passed undetected under the nose of the Germans. The worst must be over. Even Rouf seemed to sense the triumph. He was chasing his tail and he only did that these days when he was high with happiness. But Jo could not share in the general elation. He could think only of the patrols they might meet before they reached the high pastures and the hut; but worse he could not get out of his head that the Corporal had guessed what they were up to. There had been a look in his eye – he was certain of it – a knowing look. 'We must make it look like a fête, a holiday,' Papa had said. 'We don't hurry it, we enjoy it.' And so they did. They reached the plateau by lunchtime. They picnicked by the stream and the animals browsed hungrily in the lush grass. They did not wander far because they did not need to.

It was proving almost impossible to keep the cave children away from each other. Benjamin spent his time persuading them to stay with their newly adopted families, but in spite of all he could do they seemed always to gravitate to each other again. It wasn't that the language was a barrier between them and the village children — after all some of the cave children were French — but there seemed to be an instinctive reserve that kept them apart.

It was only when Hubert appeared lumbering across the stream, four children clinging to his back, that they all found a mutual source of fun that brought cave children and village children together. Hubert, the great giant, had to be hauled down and held down and it took almost all of them to do it. In the pile of children on top of him they were all allies in the one cause. Michael and Laurent clung to the same leg and were shaken off. They rolled away together giggling before returning once more to the fray.

The afternoon climb was slow. It was steep now, up along narrow, tortuous tracks, where the sheep could only move in single file. The pigs hated climbing and were forever trying to wander off, and the cows too had had enough of it now. For many of the children the adventure had lost its early magic. Their legs ached, their feet hurt, and many of them had to ride. Every donkey now — every horse — was carrying at least one child. Christine insisted on sharing a donkey with Léah. Michael's leg had lasted well until he stumbled and fell. He limped on for a bit until Hubert noticed him. He led Michael to a rock and crouched down in front of it. Michael climbed on and rode Hubert all the way up.

And so they came at long last to the high pastures, the horses first, then the sheep, the cows and last of all the reluctant pigs; and in amongst them all the hundred or so men, women and children who had brought them there. They lay down, man and beast, side by side, in silent exhaustion. They drank from the spring by the hut or from the stream that flowed from it. Michael and Jo cupped their hands in the spring and drank until they could drink no more. When Jo looked up the cave children were already being led towards the hut. 'Come on,' said Jo and they stood up.

'Is that Spain over there?' said Michael looking up at the peaks.

'That's Spain,' said Jo. They parted at the door of the hut.

'Don't lose my queen will you?' said Michael, and he went into the hut with the others.

When Jo turned round Benjamin was standing in front of him, Léah at his side. 'I'll be seeing you later then, Jo,' he said. Léah reached up and kissed him on the cheek. And then she was gone. He heard Papa's voice from inside the hut. 'Is that all of them? Have you counted them in?'

'That's all of them,' said Benjamin. 'All we've got to do now is wait until dark.'

Papa emerged from the hut and closed the door. 'You'd better get back down the mountain,' he said, and then his mouth fell open. He was looking over Jo's shoulder. Jo turned. Coming out of the trees were three soldiers. Everyone had seen them now. No-one moved. No-one said a word. There was no doubt about it, the one in front was the Corporal.

Chapter Nine

The Corporal was out of breath. 'A hard climb for an old man,' he said. 'You bring the pigs too?'

'We fatten them up on the whey,' said Papa. 'Waste not, want not.'

'Of course,' said the Corporal and he looked about him. 'Mountains,' he said. 'The transhumance. It must be the same the world over I expect; but back at home we have only the cows and horses. The horses, they are like yours except they have flaxen manes and tails – Haflingers we call them. But just like you do we take them all up to the high pastures in the summer; except of course we do not all go together.'

Papa was quick to explain – too quick, Jo thought. 'The shepherds will part them up this evening,' he said, 'and they'll take them off to their own mountainside. Every shepherd has his own mountainside.'

The Corporal nodded. 'Of course,' he said. 'Of course. Back at home,' he went on and he was looking straight at the hut as he spoke, 'back at home it is just the men who drive the animals, and their dogs of course. No women, no children. You must have almost the whole village up here.'

Hubert came running across to the Corporal and looked at him through his binoculars from a metre away. The Corporal smiled and winked into the binoculars. 'Hello Hubert,' he said, but Jo could see he was still interested in the hut. 'And you pass the whole Summer alone up here?'

Papa leaned back against the door of the hut. 'That's right,' he said.

'Do you mind if we fill our water bottles?' the Corporal asked.

'Go ahead,' said Papa.

'Hans,' said the Corporal, holding out his water bottle and pointing to the spring. He turned back to Papa. 'So you have to do all the work yourself, the milking, the shepherding, the cheesemaking.'

'Everything,' said Papa watching the soldier as he crouched beside the spring. 'I take the donkey down to the village once a week with the cheeses, pick up supplies and I'm back here in time to milk them in the evening.'

A shutter squeaked and banged open in the wind. The soldier at the spring looked up once and then looked again, his eyes squinting. He screwed the top on the water bottle and stood up, his eyes still on the shutter that swung back and forth now on its hinges. He began to walk towards it. No-one moved a muscle.

'That must be hard work,' said the Corporal, but Papa was not listening. His face was frozen. Jo could feel the queen in his pocket and squeezed it until his eyes watered. He looked up at the Corporal and their eyes met. In that moment the Corporal knew and understood. Jo was sure of it.

'Hans,' the Corporal shouted. Hans hesitated looking from the window to the Corporal and back again. 'Hans,' said the Corporal, more quietly this time. '*Kommen sie zurück. Nichts da.*' The soldier shrugged his shoulders and came back. The Corporal turned to Papa. 'You should get that mended,' he said. 'If you do not, it will blow off in the first storm.' And then he spoke to everyone. 'Lieutenant Weissmann has sent me out to escort you all back,' he said. 'We shall need to start down now I think. I am sure you know that you must be back inside your homes before curfew.'

No-one needed to be asked twice. Families gathered together briefly to say goodbye to their men and then they followed the soldiers past the piggery and the donkey shelter and made their way down towards the tree line. The last Jo saw of Papa he was standing at the door of the hut, the other shepherds around him. Jo lifted his hand to wave and then a rock was between them and he could see them no more.

With Christine on his shoulders Hubert walked beside Jo all the way down the mountain. Hardly anyone spoke. The soldiers walked on ahead of them, stopping every now and then to let them catch up. Once at the river everyone stopped to rest and Jo looked around for the Corporal. He was sitting on his own, his back to everyone, tugging at the grass beside him. Hubert went to sit beside him and showed him how he could make rude noises by blowing the grass through his thumbs. The Corporal seemed preoccupied and disinterested; and after a few moments Hubert got up and moved away to blow on his grass alone. Jo wanted to go right up to the Corporal there and then to thank him. He wanted to tell everyone what the Corporal had done. If only they knew what he knew they would be carrying him shoulder high into the village. As it was, when they got back home they all vanished into their houses bursting with the news of their success. Jo could hear it now, the same story in every house, about how the children would be over the border tonight and away, and about how they'd had a bit of luck up by the hut, but that otherwise it had all gone according to plan. And sure enough that was precisely the story Grandpère told Maman as soon as they got in.

'One look through that window,' said Grandpère, 'and that would've been that. Makes me sick just to think about it. If the Corporal hadn't picked that moment to call the soldier away then God only knows what would have happened.'

'Perhaps it was the prayer Benjamin said this morning,' said Maman.

'Maybe,' said Grandpère. Jo thought then of speaking up. He had to force himself not to. What the Corporal had done he'd done for him. It was personal and it was private and he could tell no-one, not ever.

The village always seemed an empty echoing place that first morning after the transhumance, and sad too; but the mood when Jo reached school that morning was jubilant. Everyone had been told time and again never to talk about the escape, never ever to mention it; but they still gathered in conspiratorial huddles and relived their exploits. Jo was uneasy though, and he had good cause. From dawn they'd been expecting word that the children had crossed safely over into Spain. It had all been arranged. The Widow Horcada was going to let them know just as soon as Benjamin got back. But there had been no word. 'No news is good news,' Grandpère kept saying – rather too often Jo thought.

All through first lesson that morning Jo looked out of the window and tried to convince himself that nothing could have gone wrong. After all, what could go wrong between the hut and the border? 'So close you could spit into Spain,' that's what Grandpère always said. Jo squeezed the queen in his pocket and closed his eyes for a moment. He tried to pray but he couldn't. He tried to obliterate his worst fears, but he could not. The night had been pitch black and perfect. Papa was there to guide them over. They couldn't have got lost. They'd go the silent way, walking on the grass not across the scree. There'd be someone waiting for them on the other side to take the children on into Spain. Benjamin and Papa would be back in the hut by midnight at the latest – Papa had said as much. They were going to rest for an hour or two before the descent, and Papa was going to bring Benjamin down as far as the river and let him go on back to Widow Horcada's house alone. Nothing could have gone wrong. No news was good news. Please God.

'Jo?' Monsieur Audap was coming towards his desk. 'I don't think you've been entirely with us this morning, Jo. If you've seen the view out of that window once you've seen it a thousand times. Now, whilst I appreciate you are not a natural mathematician . . .' The door burst open and Hubert was standing there, his mouth open, straining to make intelligible words out of his grunting. He was beckoning frantically. 'Stay where you are all of you,' said Monsieur Audap. 'I'll be back in a minute.' But Jo was out of the door even before he was. Hubert took his arm and ran with him down towards the Square. By the time they reached it Jo expected to find it full of the cave children, but it was empty. There were heads at every window and people standing in the street craning to look. Jo was about to run on but a hand held him back firmly. Monsieur Audap was at his side and the school children had filled the street behind him. Madame Soulet came out of her shop wiping her hands on her apron and Jo saw her look up the street and then rush back inside and shut the door. The next moment her face appeared pale in the window, and now Jo could see what she had seen.

There was a soldier in front and one on either side, and there was someone else between them but Jo still could not make out who it was. And then he knew who it was and his heart turned cold. It looked like one person at first, but it was two. Benjamin was carrying Léah, her arms around his neck, her head buried in his shoulder. He stopped now and put her down. He crouched down and straightened her coat, talking to her all the while. Then he took her hand and they walked slowly into the Square, which was filling now with silent people. From behind Jo came the sound of running boots. Lieutenant Weissmann, the Corporal and a dozen soldiers pushed their way through the school children and into the Square. Soldiers fanned out all over the Square driving the crowd back. One of the soldiers saluted as Lieutenant Weissmann came up. Jo could understand nothing of what was being said but he heard one word repeated over and over again, '*Juden*'. The Lieutenant walked across to Benjamin and looked at him and then down at Léah. 'You are Jews?' he asked.

Benjamin smiled and nodded. 'We are,' he said. 'May we sit down please? The little girl is very tired and so am I.' The Corporal pulled out two chairs from outside the café and they sat down side by side still holding hands.

Lieutenant Weissmann looked around him. 'Is Monsieur Sarthol here?' he said. Monsieur Sarthol stepped out of the crowd. 'Monsieur Sarthol,' said the Lieutenant, 'I must get these two down to the station at once. They'll never get there on foot. My horse is lame, so I will need a horse, a donkey, whatever you can find.'

Monsieur Sarthol nodded. 'You heard what the Lieutenant said,' he said. 'He needs a donkey or a horse.' No-one spoke. 'For God's sake, do you want them to have to walk?'

'They can have mine,' said Monsieur Audap, and then he turned to Jo. 'Fetch her, Jo, will you?' he said quietly. 'You know where to find her saddle.' Jo hesitated. 'Fetch her,' said Monsieur Audap, an edge to his voice.

Laurent went with him. 'What happened?' he said as they ran up the hill. 'What went wrong?'

'I don't know,' said Jo. 'I don't know.' It was all he could do to hold back his tears.

They found Monsieur Audap's mare and saddled her up together. Laurent held her mane as Jo slipped the bridle over her ears.

'What'll they do with them?' said Laurent.

'One of those camps,' said Jo.

The crowd parted as they led the horse into the Square. Benjamin was talking urgently to Léah, smoothing her hair. They looked up and saw Jo coming towards them. Neither showed any flicker of recognition. Jo held the horse as Benjamin mounted from a chair. The Corporal handed Léah up to him and she sat clutching the mane, Benjamin's arm around her.

'You'll be escorted to the train by the Corporal,' said the Lieutenant.

'And after that?' said Benjamin.

'That is not my concern,' said the Lieutenant and he stepped aside.

A soldier took the reins from Jo. Jo looked up at Benjamin who held out his hand. '*Dziękuję,*' he said. Jo took his hand. '*Dziękuję,*' Benjamin said again. For a moment Léah's eyes met Jo's and held them.

The Lieutenant was frowning at him. 'Do you know them?' he said. Jo shook his head.

'Of course not,' said Benjamin. 'We know no-one here and no-one knows us. The boy brought me a horse and I simply said thank you. Is it not permitted for a Jew even to say thank you?'

Jo watched them being led away, the horse's hooves slipping on the cobbles as she was led across the Square, down the hill and out of sight. Monsieur Audap tried to gather the children together and take them back to school; but many, like Jo, drifted away homewards. As he walked home through the empty streets he gleaned from the squeeze of Benjamin's hand, from the single word Benjamin had been able to say to him, all that he had wanted to say and was not able to say without betraying him.

The news had reached home before him. Papa was sitting hunched over the table, head in his hands. He looked up as Jo came in, his eyes full of tears. 'You mustn't go blaming yourself,' said Maman. She prised his hands away from his face and kissed them. 'We all did what we could, everyone did.'

'Did we?' said Grandpère fiercely. 'I was in the Square just now. There were over a hundred of us and just twenty-two of them – and we just stood and watched them take them away.' He looked away to hide his face.

'What happened, Papa?' said Jo. 'The children, did they get away?'

'Oh yes,' said Papa, 'we got them away just like we planned. Like clockwork it was. We were up at the border before midnight. Only one thing went wrong. The little girl.'

'Léah,' said Grandpère.

'She wouldn't leave him,' Papa went on. 'I tell you, Jo, I've never seen anything like it. The strength of the girl. There wasn't much of her but she clung to Benjamin like she would drown if she let go. So we had to bring her back with us to the hut – there was nothing else we could do. Even then we weren't too unhappy. We had a glass together in the hut, Benjamin and me, to celebrate it was, before we came down. The little girl was tired of course, so I sat her on the donkey and we set off.' He drank down his glass and wiped his mouth with the back of his hand. 'But then it happened. I thought it was a boar. There was a sort of snorting, growling. You couldn't see anything, not at first.

It's funny though, Benjamin seemed to know at once what it was, almost like he was expecting it. He shouted some sort of warning to the little girl. I don't know what he said, but I understood soon enough when that bear came lumbering out of the trees. He came right at us. Benjamin stood his ground and faced him, but the donkey took off, the little girl screaming loud enough to wake the dead. I was running like the donkey was. You don't stand and fight a bear; but when I turned round I saw Benjamin throwing stones at it and shouting at it and the bear was backing away. I couldn't believe it and then I remembered all about that bear cub you told me about, the one that Benjamin brought up, and I put two and two together; so I started throwing stones at him too. He was up on his hind legs and waving his paws like he was boxing and we were hitting him again and again and still he came on. Then it seemed like he'd had enough of it and he went down on all fours and just walked off. All the time we could hear the little girl crying and screaming somewhere behind us and the donkey braying down in the valley. I went after the donkey, Benjamin went after the little girl.' Papa shook his head. 'I should never have left him. I should never have left him. I was gone a few minutes. Took me a bit of time to calm the donkey down. I was leading him back up through the trees towards them. The little girl, she was still crying like she would never stop and he was trying to comfort her. Then suddenly there were torchlights and shouting and there were soldiers everywhere. And what did I do? I crouched there in the darkness like a frightened rabbit, that's what I did. And I stayed there until I was sure they had gone. What does that make me, eh? You've a coward for a father, Jo.'

Jo put out his hand to touch Papa's shoulder. 'He said "thankyou",' said Jo. 'Benjamin, he said to thank you.' Papa looked away.

'Someone's got to go up there and tell Alice,' said Grandpère, 'and I don't know if I can, not on my own.'

'I'll come,' Maman said, standing up and wrapping her shawl about her. 'Jo, you can stay here and look after your sister.' She put her arms around Papa's neck and kissed him on top of the head. 'You'd better get yourself back up the mountain, those sheep won't milk themselves.' She took Grandpère's arm. 'Come on,' she said. 'Let's get this over with.'

In the days that followed the exodus of the cave children an unseasonal fog settled over the village and it matched perfectly the mood of the place. Yet even when it cleared and they began to cut the hay the village seemed incapable of lifting itself out of its gloom, and that in spite of the news of the war. It was all good. France was being liberated from the north and from the south too. The end of the occupation could not be far off now, but few in Lescun could rejoice in it.

No-one spoke to the German soldiers any more. When people saw them coming they turned their backs and walked away. The soldiers scarcely ever ventured into the café and if they did they were met with a hostile silence that soon drove them out. There was no more nostalgic talk of old battles, no more sweets for the children.

Jo did all he could to avoid the Corporal, not because he blamed him for what had happened to Benjamin or Léah – he knew that was none of the Corporal's doing – but because he had come at last to see him as a man in the uniform of the enemy, a good and kindly man Jo had no doubt of that, but nonetheless an enemy too. It was a confusion he did not wish to confront. Their eyes met several times across the street but they never spoke, not until the evening Jo ran into the church porch to escape a torrential downpour, his jacket over his head. When he pulled it off he saw the Corporal standing beside him in the shadows.

'Hello Jo,' he said. Jo made to move away. 'No-one can see us, Jo.' The Corporal took off his cap and shook it. 'Hubert gave me back the binoculars.'

'I know,' Jo said.

'But the little cup he made, I shall keep it. I shall take it home when this is over, and it will not be long now I think. It will remind me of this place, of him, of you.'

'They were taken to one of those camps, weren't they?' said Jo. The Corporal said nothing.

'But why?' said Jo, 'What for? What did they do?' The Corporal took a deep breath and let it out slowly. 'I have no answers, Jo,' he said. 'I know no answers, no reasons. I have thought much of that man and the little girl, and still I do not understand.'

'He was a friend of mine,' said Jo fiercely. 'They both were. He was hiding up in the mountains, and do you know why? He was waiting for his daughter to come so they could escape together into Spain. He wouldn't leave without her.'

'The little girl, she was his daughter?'

'That was Léah,' said Jo. 'His daughter's called Anya. He was so sure she would come, but she never did.' The Corporal put on his cap and made to move away. 'That day up at the hut,' Jo went on. 'You knew, didn't you?'

The Corporal nodded. 'I thought there was someone inside,' he said, 'someone or maybe something you did not want me to see.'

'There was,' said Jo. 'There were twelve Jewish children, and they escaped. All except Léah, they escaped.' And he did not try to disguise the triumph in his voice.

'Well, well,' said the Corporal. 'I suppose that's something. *Auf Wiedersehen* Jo.' And pulling up the collar of his coat he walked out into the rain.

They were carting in the hay a few days later when Jo thought he heard the sound of distant thunder. Maman brought the horse to a halt and Grandpère held up his hand. It wasn't thunder, it was drumming. It was Hubert drumming. Christine screamed at being left behind but Jo ran on ahead anyway. As he ran down through the streets he was aware there were others running with him, all around him now; and the drumming echoed off the walls of the houses so that it seemed as if Hubert must be beating a dozen drums. In the Square they were all hugging each other and crying. 'They've gone!' Jo heard. 'The Germans have gone!'

The bells were ringing and Monsieur Sarthol was leaning out of the window of the Mairie and fumbling with a faded tricolour that would not run out on its pole, but when it did it was greeted with such a din of clapping and cheering that Jo couldn't hear what Laurent was shouting in his ear, not at first. 'Hubert!' he shouted, 'look at Hubert!' Outside the café they were drinking straight from the bottles, arms around each other and dancing; and Hubert was standing by his drum and drinking wine as if it were water. He finished the bottle and raised his hands in the air, laughing till the tears ran down his face. When Jo saw him next he was dancing around the Square with Christine, it was a wild gallop more than a dance but Christine was loving it.

Monsieur Sarthol stood on the war memorial and tried to make a speech but no-one would listen so he gave up and sang the Marseillaise instead, bottle in hand. By the end of it everyone was linking arms and singing with him. Then Father Lasalle was running in amongst them. 'Quick!' he shouted, tugging Monsieur Sarthol by the arm. 'Quick! It's Hubert, he's in the churchyard. I think he's gone mad. He's trying to push away one of the tombstones.' And Jo knew at once which tombstone.

He was there before anyone. The tombstone was ajar and Hubert was nowhere to be seen. He didn't need to look in to see if Grandpère's rifle was still there. It would be gone, he knew it. From the graveyard wall he could see Hubert springing down the hillside, the rifle held above his head; and on the winding track below the village the grey column of German soldiers led by Lieutenant Weissmann on his horse. 'Don't Hubert! Don't!' he called, and he saw Lieutenant Weissmann swivel in his saddle and look upwards. 'Don't shoot!' Jo cried. 'Don't shoot!' Hubert had stopped. He was aiming the rifle at the soldiers. Jo vaulted the wall and ran screaming down the hill waving his hands. He leapt the ditch and blundered through the hedges and all the while he called out, 'Hubert! Hubert! Don't! Don't!'

He never saw the shooting, he tripped over a root and was picking himself up when he heard it. There were just two shots. He looked where Hubert had been and could not see him.

Lieutenant Weissmann was running up the hill towards him, a pistol in his hand. Jo found Hubert lying on his back in the long grass, the rifle still grasped in his hand. His eyes were looking at the sun but not seeing. Jo looked at the blood on the grass by his shoe and thought of the bear lying stretched out on the chairs in the Square all those years before. The blood of a man was the same red as the blood of a bear. A shadow came over him and he looked up. Lieutenant Weissmann was looking down at him. He crouched down beside Hubert and felt his neck. 'A pity,' he said and he stood up. 'I am sorry, very sorry.'

'He didn't mean it,' said Jo as the Lieutenant walked away; and then he was shouting after him. 'He didn't mean it! He didn't mean it . . .'

* * *

A few months later the war was over. The men from the prisoner-of-war camps came home, or most of them did. Everyone waited for some word of Benjamin and Léah, but there was no word; instead came the first dreadful rumours, rumours that there were some camps – concentration camps – where Jews and others had been systematically murdered. Even when there were pictures in the newspapers and reports on the wireless Widow Horcada refused to believe it. Jo clung to Benjamin's own maxim: 'Wait and pray,' he had said 'Wait and pray'; but often alone in the cold church he would cry into his hands, for he somehow knew that his prayers were too late.

Meanwhile Monsieur Audap had been making enquiries. It seemed that Benjamin and Léah had been taken first to Gurs concentration camp about thirty kilometres away. From there they had been sent on to Auschwitz. Auschwitz was a death camp, he said. There were only a few survivors, and

Benjamin and Léah were not amongst them. Like millions of Jews they would not be coming home.

Grandpère broke the news to Widow Horcada and was a constant source of comfort through her dark and grieving days. It was to no-one's great surprise when the two of them got married just before the Winter snows set in. Grandpère moved out of the house 'to start all over again' as he put it, up at Widow Horcada's farm. He took the pigs with him and that pleased Papa who could never take to them.

Jo left school the next Summer and became a full-time shepherd. With only Rouf for company he took the sheep up to the mountains and lived in the hut as Papa and Grandpère had done before him. Rouf was all the company he needed or sought. He buried himself in his work – it was the only way to forget the gnawing pain inside him. But at nights asleep in his hut the faces of Hubert, Benjamin and Léah haunted his dreams.

One Sunday afternoon, with the cheesemaking done, Jo was resting on his bed with Rouf beside him. It was the dog who heard the voices first and lifted his head. Then Jo heard Papa coughing and Christine prattling on. They often came up on a Sunday for a picnic. Jo had to steel himself to be sociable. Papa would question him endlessly about the sheep and Christine would want her ride on the donkey. He was surprised though when he heard Widow Horcada's voice too. He swung his legs off the bed as Grandpère put his head round the door.

'Not disturbing you are we?' he said.

Jo blinked in the bright sunlight and held his hand over his eyes so that he could see better. They were all there. Papa was helping Widow Horcada down from her horse and Maman had the picnic basket on her arm. Rouf was greeting Christine in his usual boisterous way, paws on her shoulders. She staggered back and sat down hard, Rouf on top of her. She laughed and everyone laughed.

'Well, Jo,' said Widow Horcada shaking out her skirts. 'Have you lost your tongue? Don't you know how to say hello to strangers?'

'Strangers?' said Jo.

And then he saw the girl. She was walking towards him. She had red hair that she pushed back out of her eyes and tucked behind her ears.

'I'm Anya,' she said.

Michael Morpurgo

MR NOBODY'S EYES

"'Are you arguing with me?' Her lips were tight with fury. 'Are You?' 'No Miss.'

Harry knew he was stupid to have started it, but he would not let anyone call Bill his father, not even The Dragon."

Nothing has ever been the same for Harry since his mother remarried. With the new baby at home and only trouble at school, life is unbearable. When Ocky, the chimp, escapes from the circus, Harry decides to join his only friend in the world and together they run away.

Michael Morpurgo has written many novels, including *King of the Cloud Forests*, commended for the Carnegie Medal, *My Friend Walter*, shortlisted for the Smarties Prize, and the highly acclaimed *Why The Whales Came* which was made into a major feature film.

Michael Morpurgo

WAR HORSE

It is 1914. In England, Albert is growing up on a Devon farm with a young horse he calls Joey. In Germany, Friedrich works in his butcher's shop. In France, Emilie and her brothers play in their orchard. But the clouds of war are on the horizon and great armies are gathering their strength. Soon they will all be drawn into the nightmare of battle.

This is the story of Joey and the people whose lives he touches, as they struggle for survival in the blasted wilderness of the Western Front.

A Selected List of Fiction from Mammoth

While every effort is made to keep prices low, it is sometimes necessary to increase prices at short notice. Mandarin Paperbacks reserves the right to show new retail prices on covers which may differ from those previously advertised in the text or elsewhere.

The prices shown below were correct at the time of going to press.

☐	7497 0978 2	**Trial of Anna Cotman**	Vivien Alcock	£2.99
☐	7497 1510 3	**A Map of Nowhere**	Gillian Cross	£2.99
☐	7497 1066 7	**The Animals of Farthing Wood**	Colin Dann	£3.99
☐	7497 0914 6	**Follyfoot**	Monica Dickens	£2.99
☐	7497 0184 6	**The Summer House Loon**	Anne Fine	£2.99
☐	7497 0443 8	**Fast From the Gate**	Michael Hardcastle	£2.50
☐	7497 1784 X	**Listen to the Dark**	Maeve Henry	£2.99
☐	7497 0136 6	**I Am David**	Anne Holm	£3.50
☐	7497 1473 5	**Charmed Life**	Diana Wynne Jones	£3.50
☐	7497 1664 9	**Hiding Out**	Elizabeth Laird	£2.99
☐	7497 0791 7	**The Ghost of Thomas Kempe**	Penelope Lively	£2.99
☐	7497 0634 1	**Waiting for Anya**	Michael Morpurgo	£2.99
☐	7497 0831 X	**The Snow Spider**	Jenny Nimmo	£2.99
☐	7497 0412 8	**Voices of Danger**	Alick Rowe	£2.99
☐	7497 0410 1	**Space Demons**	Gillian Rubinstein	£2.99
☐	7497 0656 2	**Journey of 1000 Miles**	Ian Strachan	£2.99
☐	7497 0796 8	**Kingdom by the Sea**	Robert Westall	£2.99

All these books are available at your bookshop or newsagent, or can be ordered direct from the address below. Just tick the titles you want and fill in the form below.

Cash Sales Department, PO Box 5, Rushden, Northants NN10 6YX.
Fax: 01933 414047 : Phone: 01933 414000.

Please send cheque, payable to 'Reed Book Services Ltd.', or postal order for purchase price quoted and allow the following for postage and packing:

＾for the first book, 50p for the second; **FREE POSTAGE AND PACKING FOR THREE BOOKS OR** ＾PER ORDER.

＾ock letters) ....

＾DRESS ....

....

☐ I enclose my remittance for ....

☐ I wish to pay by Access/Visa Card Number

Expiry Date

Signature ....

Please quote our reference: MAND